GOING THE DISTANCE FOR MY HITTA

TAJA MORGAN

Going the Distance for My Hitta
Copyright 2020 by Taja Morgan

Published by Mz. Lady P Presents, LLC

All rights reserved

This book is a work of fiction. Names, characters, places, and incidents either are the product of the author's imagination or are used fictitiously and are not to be construed as real. Any resemblance to actual persons, living or dead, business establishments, events, or locales or, is entirely coincidental.

No portion of this book may be used or reproduced in any manner whatsoever without writer permission except in the case of brief quotations embodied in critical articles and reviews.

Keep Up With Taja

Instagram: Taja Writes

Facebook: Taja Morgan/Taja Writes

1

Billi Samuels

"I'on even know why I allowed you to even talk my ass into coming here."

Nomi and I had been tight at the hip since back in grade school. I guess it's safe to say we bonded over our issues as young girls, which indeed bonded us closer, almost as if we were blood related.

Fast forward to the present, and nothing changed much except for our age. To say we were from the harshest city in all of Louisiana, our upbringing wasn't quite what the typical New Orleans native would expect. We were coddled our whole lives and protected from the streets. According to our mothers, especially since they were the best of friends, neither one of them wanted their baby girls being products of the streets.

I found it quite ironic how mama tried to escape from the one thing she attracted back in her day. Due to my father's foolish decisions, he's lost out on his freedom and would spend the rest of his life behind bars. Mama never really fully disclosed what happened, but I do know she did whatever she had to do to ensure her only child had the best life possible.

"You need some damn excitement in your life. By that, I don't mean running the streets with Joey's trifling ass. Speaking of, you need to go ahead and leave that trash where it's at, B. On the real."

Nomi's naturally beautiful. Her golden skin and perfect sized assets would cause the average nigga to fall to their knees. She was truly blessed with an attraction far out of this world, due to her Creole roots. Despite her physical attractiveness, she had the brains as well. After knocking it out of the park in nursing school, she now worked as an ER nurse and was slowly making her come up in this harsh world.

"Ain't shit going is on between him and me that you don't already know about. It ain't like I plan on spending my entire ass life with the nigga. I just want dick, with no strings attached."

As mature women, we had the choice to be spending this Friday night sweating out our best bundles in some club, but we took the better approach with a simple, upscale dinner. This was right up Nomi's bougie ass alley. In her eyes, nothing was ever too damn expensive. She felt the need to live the high life because she worked hard for it, and I had to hand it to my girl, she was right.

We spent the entire week working our ass off. She did her thing with nursing. Meanwhile, I kept a low profile with my nail technician business.

As the child of a celebrity stylist who's rubbed elbows with damn near every soul in the industry, everyone expected me to follow in her footsteps or become a better version of her. Unfortunately, I rebelled against her parenting so much until it's driven a wedge between us. In my opinion, along with the fame, my mother became way too Hollywood, completely forgetting where she'd come from.

For months, I'd been on my own in New Orleans in search of something practically anything to give myself the head start to make a name for myself. With no need for college, I missed out on what could've been the best moments of my life. Overall, none of that could amount to moving back home to be with my best friend.

"Enough about me, you need to start planning for this wedding, soon to be Mrs. Knighten."

"Not you too." Nomi sighed, shaking her head. "Don't get me wrong, the thought of being a wife is amazing, and I love being a fiancée, but the planning and everything is not doing a damn thing except stressing me out."

"Don't talk like that. You're engaged to the love of your life, Nomi. What's with the dramatics?"

"I love Yadriel with everything in me. I enjoy the thought of us spending a life together and all, but…I'on know. I guess I'm just having cold feet plus this bullshit with his folks and mine not getting along. It's stressful. I haven't told anyone about this yet, not even Dri, but I'm thinking about taking a leave from work to go back to school," she confided. "The hospital is just way too much for me, and with the planning, it's starting to fuck with me. I know mama's gonna go the fuck off, but I feel like I'm drowning."

"You know I'll always support whatever you do, no matter what. Do what you feel is needed, and I'm right behind you. I'm sure Dri will understand. Hell, he's doing the damn thing with his artistry, so I know he won't have a problem with holding you down." I smiled, grabbing her hand. "Hey girl, don't beat yourself up. Just talk to him and go with your move. That's all you can do."

To say Nomi was successful as she was, she had a

serious bout of insecurities and her need for wanting to make those around incredibly proud. On the outside looking in, she had it all.

We were both one and the same, damn near. I was only twenty-three, and with no support from my mother, I had no other choice but to do it on my own.

You see, that's the negative aspect of adulting. When you make a mistake, you fall on your ass and expected to get right back up. In this life, you never really know your true outcome, but if it's one thing I learned, it was to always keep going.

Retiring home to my condo, you'd think with being here for months, I'd get used to it, but I wasn't. I sometimes enjoy isolation and being on my own, but Nomi has been my right hand since moving back to New Orleans. My girl was getting married and due to move out of the duplex we shared soon. She'd stay at Yadriel's certain nights, and I'd be left on my own, alone with my thoughts.

Stepping onto the elevator, my eyes were glued to the screen of my phone as I entertained the stupidity in my messages. Glancing up, a stranger stepped on before the doors closed. With a black hoodie covering his face, his shoulder-length locs peeked from underneath the hood, and he kept his face stared down at the floor and into his phone.

Before I could even pay any mind to his face, my phone started to vibrate with an incoming call, causing me to roll my eyes.

"I'm not in the mood for your bullshit. Not tonight."

"A nigga ain't trying to hear all'at right now. Yo, where you at?"

"Oh, the fuck no, come correct. Don't call me demanding shit nigga, bye."

Thankfully, the elevator stopped on my floor, and to my surprise, I hadn't even noticed the guy stepped off as well.

Sorely needing a bubble bath accompanied by my favorite wine, I didn't waste any time entering my condo. This place started to feel more and more empty, the more I began to realize Nomi would be gone for good. There was no way I could afford this shit on my own, so I'd need to downsize.

Throwing my keys onto the desk nearby, I locked up and traveled into the kitchen where the mail sat. Not even bothering to sort through it, I reached into the wine fridge and grabbed my bottle with a wine glass. Pouring the remaining remnants into my glass, I then traveled upstairs to my bedroom to undress and then towards the bathroom to begin running my water.

The vibration of my phone abruptly started up once again as I rolled my eyes. Joey's name was plastered onto the screen.

"You must want me to hang up on your ass again, don't you?"

"I'm outside your door, B."

Going against my better judgment, I hung up and pulled on my robe while heading to answer the door. Unlocking each lock, I opened the door, and there he stood. With that hot boy, stupid ass smile all over his face, I noticed the bouquet of roses in his hands while he entered.

"You could've at least called me to let me know you were in town."

"What's the point of a surprise if I told you?" he questioned, stepping closer and grabbing my waist. "I missed you."

Every bitch on this planet had their personal bad habit. For me, it just so happened to be suave ass, Joey. Originally, from Los Angeles, he was a well-known rapper up and throughout the South, mainly for his lyrical abilities. With cocoa skin as smooth as your finest piece of chocolate, he was a looker. Various tattoos covered the majority of his body, and his well-kempt fade meshed well with his trimmed facial hair.

Jumping into his arms, we made our way to the sectional, where I couldn't keep my hands off of him. Our lips moved in an undeniable sync, mainly stemmed by the lust between us and how much I've missed him. His career was the main reason for his extreme traveling, but whenever he was on my side of town, he always made sure to show me a good time.

"Where's Nomi?"

"At Yadriel's so, I have the house to myself for the night. Speaking of such, I need to catch my water before it overflows. You wanna join me?"

"Lead the way."

It could all be so simple to live a happy life with a good man on my arms and family who supported me, but it was all just simple figments of my imagination. My fucked up reality managed to tarnish those dreams way before they could be mended. Fortunately, I was living, but not how I should.

"I was out in New York and crossed paths with your mother," Joey stated, breaking the silence. Submerged in the tub, my back was against his chest as I sipped on my wine, and his arms wrapped around my waist. "She told me y'all hadn't talked since August."

"Sounds about right."

"Come on now, Billi. That's your moms. I've been telling you to take it easy with this angry ass attitude."

"Oh well. There are more things to be worried about in life and worrying about my mother ain't one of them."

2

Kenji Breaux

The betrayal of my body hit at an all-time high once last night's events replayed themselves in my mind. The aches, bruises, and pains were all the reminder I needed that maybe, just maybe I needed to hang up my bad habit.

I'd been called every single name in the book. The exterior I've grown over time has hardened to the point where words no longer fazed me. Over the years, I've mastered the art of remaining emotionless even during some of the harshest, most tragic moments experienced throughout my twenty-five years of living. As sad as it sounds, I can't even remember the last time I shed a tear, let alone had a damn good laugh because I was only living.

Stepping in the steaming shower, the water fell onto my body, soothing the soreness. The bruises were now a darkened shade of purple, but thankfully, my face managed to be unscathed.

After a well-needed shower, I figured it'd be best to get a start on my morning. The early morning jog loosened me up, and after popping a few Advil, the pain was bearable but not too much that I couldn't handle. My everyday breakfast consisted of turkey bacon, egg whites, oatmeal, and fresh fruit; no sugary ass coffee included. Water and my vitamins added just enough for me to remain balanced throughout the day.

Enjoying the peace while chowing down before a day's work, yelling from outside managed to capture my attention. Shaking my head, the shit was typical on this floor with whoever stayed next door.

I'd been here long enough to know whoever the nigga she was talking to must've had patience because there was no way in hell I was allowing no bitch to talk to me any kind of way. Luckily, the ringing of my phone drowned out the neighbor's yelling. Seeing my sister's name plastered on the screen, it'd be best to answer before she blew me up.

"Yes, ma'am."

"Boy, don't answer the phone all proper and shit. Fuck you doing?"

"Aye, watch yo mouth. I'm still the oldest, and you getting too comfortable with the cussing, but I'm eating."

"I tried calling last night, but…."

As the younger sibling, Ameera made it extremely hard for a nigga just to breathe without her adding her two cents. We were only three years apart, yet she felt like she was the alpha and omega. I couldn't blame her, though, because the roles are reversed when she's in harm's way. I wouldn't think twice about bodying a nigga or a bitch over my little sister.

Ameera was in her own lane, though. I was proud she'd taken the road less traveled and actually took time with doing something productive in her life. Attending college out of state is what she felt she needed to, and currently, baby girl had just successfully completed her first semester as a senior at Truth University, an HBCU located in Houston, Texas. In a big city, she was soaring with no problems whatsoever, and I couldn't be prouder.

"Daddy tells me you're still fighting."

"I gotta make money some kind of way, Meera. If you gonna come at me with all that heat and shit, I'ma tell you right now, I'm not in the mood. I had a long night and an even longer day ahead of me."

"Does it really have to amount to this, Kenj?"

"Yo, what the fuck I just say, man? You and your pops got that shit bad! Stop pressing me, especially when y'all know how I am. Why is that shit so hard?"

"Ain't no reason for you to be popping off, so calm down! Your black ass needs a reality check before you end up hurt or worse, Kenji. Look, it's apparent you're in a shitty mood, so forget I even called, and oh yeah, happy fuckin' birthday."

"KEEP THEM BOTTLES COMING, baby girl! We gotta do it up big for the homie's G day."

Leave it up to my homeboy, Apollo, to go all out with the doing the most for just another day. I should've known he had something up his sleeve when he called, but part of me needed the distraction.

You see, Apollo and I were brothers, although we lacked a true blood relation, he's been in my corner for years. He was a hood nigga through and through. We were given different aspects of the world and let's just say my nigga wanted it all and then some. He'd recently taken over his father's drug business and had become the hottest to ever do it. Damn near everybody respected his ass, but at the end of the day, he was simply a businessman doing what was needed to make a living for his folks.

Some time ago, I called myself trying my luck with the shit, but the drug game wasn't for a nigga such as myself. Often times, Apollo called my ass square because I attended college and shit, but in a way, we were cut from the same cloth. My choice of income was also illegal, but I would much rather continue with doing something I felt comfortable doing as opposed to risking my livelihood producing poison onto the streets.

"Damn, nigga, even when I get yo black ass outta the house you still on the bougie boy ass shit!"

"I'on get the point of this shit. You see the same dusty ass bitches, the same broke ass niggas and all for what? None of these mothafuckas are worth looking at, to be honest."

"What the real issue is, bro, come on and talk to me."

"Shit, ain't nothing wrong." I shrugged. "This shit just don't faze me like it used to, man. That's what's wrong with the city now. Too many people trying to impress the next mothafucka when they shit ain't even all the way together."

"K, neither one of us had the best life coming up. Man them days we spent wishing for shit like this is here, nigga! Live it the fuck up. You only live fuckin' once. Around this time, thirteen years ago, we both were looking for something to shake. This the shit we fuckin' deserve."

"A'ight Peter Popoff, I hear you. I'ma need you to hold off on them there drinks too, potnah before you end up being carried on outta here!"

Apollo's words did nothing, but whenever he consumed alcohol, he felt like he was a motivational speaker getting paid by the second. I appreciated the kind gesture, but this lifestyle he lived differed completely from mine. I'd much rather spend my night plotting on my next move as opposed to getting shit faced and disliking the fact that I'd made the stupid decision the following day.

Needing some fresh air, I took a step away from the scene and made my way out of the club. Finally, able to hear myself think, let alone have a breath of fresh air, I just stood embracing it all.

"Kenji, is that you?"

Following the sound of the soft voice, an instant irritation plagued me, but due to the ingestion of one too many shots of Cîroc, her presence was turning a nigga on.

"What's up, Erial?"

From time to time, a nigga needed an excuse to bust a nut, and despite the many women I've gone through, Erial had to be in the top two, and not even two. Something about her hood ass ways and the way she worked that pussy put a nigga in a trance. A bad bitch with a mouthpiece on her and who knew how to tame my ass just so happened to be my weakness. Her caramel toned skin was covered in tattoos, and her assets were busting out of the black dress, but it hugged her perfectly.

"I'on know, you tell me."

Sauntering her way over to me, I could smell her perfume. Placing her small tatted fingers onto my chest, she proceeded to run her fingers through my locs while biting her lip. "I've been missing you. What you doing out this way?"

"When do I ever tell you what I got going on, E?"

"You always gotta be a smart ass nigga…but that's what I like about you. I'm in town for a bit after coming down from New York. What you getting into tonight?"

"Shit, it might be you if you play your cards right."

Truth be told, I ain't even want no ass, but some head would do the trick. She saw the look in my eyes, and without hesitation, we went to the parking lot. I didn't protest nor speak a word as we entered her Benz, but once her lips wrapped around my dick, it was all she wrote.

Like I said once before, bad bitches were my weakness, and Erial had it. She just didn't have it to the point where it'd make a nigga want to wife her. She sucked a mean ass dick, though. I think it's the only reason I really ever kept her around, but the bitch was too in the business of claiming me when I didn't want to be claimed.

By the time she finished, I had thought I ain't want no ass, but she got a nigga geared up to the point where pussy wouldn't hurt either. I had some pent up anger I'd been holding in for a minute. Rolling on protection, the way I was currently killing her shit, I knew it'd be a murder scene if I went any harder.

"Oh shit, baby!" she shouted, holding onto the passenger seat. "Kenji, you gonna make me cum! Ohhh, fuck!"

I didn't do much of no talking when I fucked, strictly because a fuck was simply just a fuck. No emotions were held nor needed to be expressed, all I needed was my nut, and I was straight. Delivering a powerful slap to her ass, she tried her best to match my rhythm, but I had her ass speaking in tongues the deeper I went.

Her tinted windows turned foggy, and within seconds, her legs began to shake. The arch in her back was no longer as the warmth of her juices flowing coated the condom protecting my dick. I was a smart nigga. I rarely ever fucked raw, but with this bitch, you had to be careful, or she'd be quick to pin a bastard ass baby on a nigga.

Busting my nut, I felt accomplished. By the time I finished with her ass, she was out of breath and satisfied with that look in her eyes. Paying it no mind, I fixed my clothing until her ringing phone had caught my attention.

"Relax, it's just my homegirl. She's probably looking for me." She sighed, answering. "Yeah, Billi, I'm here…"

Taking that as the opportunity to get the fuck on, I straightened myself up. Pretty much over the party scene, I retrieved the keys from my pocket to my Audi. Walking over, my phone started to ring with an incoming call from Erial as I declined. Hearing what sounded to be like a heated argument between a woman and a nigga, I turned to the entrance of the club, seeing the woman damn near about to beat the fuck out of dude.

She had heart to be going against this big nigga, but shorty was way too little for dude to even be talking to her the way she was. Her full lips were twisted into a scowl, but when I saw him reaching for his piece, I know I needed to step in before her brains ended out on this concrete.

"Whoa, whoa, my nigga, we got a mothafuckin' problem?"

Opening his mouth to spit some hot shit, he froze when he noticed who I was. It didn't take much for me see this was one of Apollo's reckless ass street niggas. His name was Junebug, and his big ass did too much talking for me, which is why I rarely fucked with any of Apollo's crew.

"Oh, you ain't got shit to say now, do you, bitch?" the girl shouted. "But I was all types of mothafuckin' bitches and hoes just a second ago! I'll body yo big, sloppy ass in a minute with my fuckin' eyes closed—"

"It ain't gonna be all of that," I interjected, turning to him. "Now you listen to me, and you listen to me fuckin' good, you stupid ass fuck. If I ever in my mothafuckin' life catch you badmouthing or even threatening another female again, I'ma personally do the honor of escorting your mother down the aisle to your funeral, nigga. A'ight?"

Steaming with anger, he looked back at her, and I could see the emotion in his face, but he and I both knew this could end one of two ways. Taking the higher road, he returned inside and went on his way as the girl let out an irritating chuckle, following by a sigh.

Even at her angriest, she was beautiful. She wasn't usually the type I'd go for, but for some reason, I couldn't take my eyes off of her, and that's where it hit me, she was the girl from my building.

"I appreciate that, but I could've handled him myself, thank you very much."

"I ain't say you couldn't, but I'm a man, and as long as I'm standing, I'm not about to allow some nigga to threaten and throw shots at a lady when I'm capable of diffusing the situation. What's your name?"

"We've met before."

"Nah, we've seen each other, but never been properly introduced. And I asked you a question that you have yet to answer."

"Billi."

"Well, Billi, do you need a ride? My whip is right over there, and we stay in the same building. It's the least I could do."

"You honestly think I'm about to get in a car with you? I'on know your name and don't think I'on notice how fucked up you be when you get in at night. What do you do? You a fuckin' assassin or some shit?"

"You real fuckin' nosey, you know that?"

"As nosey as you are thirsty," she replied, cocking her eyebrow.

"I'm an underground boxer, ma. It's not the shabbiest source of income, but it works for me. Now you got any more questions or you about to take this ride because that offer can switch up real quick, and it's colder than a moth-afucka out here, so take your pick."

"A'ight, cool. Lead the way."

3

Billi

There was nothing in the world that I hated more than a disrespectful ass bitch. Here this hostess ass hoe didn't even know if this was my man or not, yet she been flirting hard as fuck since the moment she seated us. I wasn't the one to judge, but I highly doubt a bitch that worked at **IHOP** was up Kenji's alley, but I was willing to be cordial because I barely even knew this man. The absolute last thing I needed was him thinking I was a person who loved negativity.

"You've been quiet ever since ol' girl seated us," Kenji stated. "You good?"

"Our hostess has been flirting with you the moment you walked in here, and you haven't paid her no mind. I find it funny that she's still trying hard as hell, and your rude ass is acting like you don't know she sees something she wants."

"The fuck I'ma do with a hoe that works at IHOP?" He laughed, bucking his eyes. "I'ma be respectful because she's holding my food and I'on trust the bitch, but that mothafucka ain't got nothing I want."

"Remind me to always stay on your good side because something tells me your mouth is lethal."

"Oh shit, look who's talking."

"Okay, look, this is not about me, sir." I chuckled, glancing at him. "So, what exactly is your story? You single?"

"Do I look like I'm single?"

"Come on, negro, don't be an ass."

"Yeah." He nodded with a slick smile. "I'm very single. Why, you must wanna fuck me?"

Choking on my orange juice, I should've expected his fine ass to be this straightforward, but I truly didn't see that coming. Bringing attention to our table due to my coughing and his laughing, I had to calm myself down and drink some of my water with a sigh.

"Come on now, we both grown," he continued shrugging. "I guarantee you that nigga you with now ain't even half of me. I'on even know why you sitting up here acting like we in high school or some shit."

"You're trouble, aren't you?"

Taking a sip from his iced water, he didn't say much but just kept those dark brown eyes on me. Damn, this nigga knew he was the shit. Cockiness stemmed from him, most definitely making it harder to ignore his advances. I had a bad habit of going from the men I know I needed to stay away from, and something just screamed that simply ignoring him wouldn't be the easiest thing.

"You think I am?"

"I was taught never to judge a book by its cover. Then again, there is something about you that I just can't put my finger on."

"And what might that be?"

"I'on wanna say too much too soon because you may shock me."

Truth be told, I needed a real ass distraction. Things between Joey and I weren't so good, and all the signs showing that I needed to leave him alone just seemed to become stronger by the day. I always vowed to remain true to what I needed as opposed to what I wanted, but like the fucked-up soul that I am, those wants just started to get way too overbearing to try to ignore.

"You seem like the type to only keep a nigga around when you're ready to be bothered. Lemme ask you something."

"I'm all ears."

"When's the last time you took a chance with doing some shit out of the ordinary?"

"I don't quite know what you mean. Please explain further."

Expressing no words, he continued to stare with this particular look in his eyes. He was hungry, but it wasn't for this food sitting in front of us. Licking his lips, the hostess returned, and he asked for the check.

Taking notice of how suave he was, I know for a fact that I needed to stay away. Men of his caliber were dangerously capable of having you fall quick and without warning. Then once you finally get a piece of the dick, you're addicted and there's no stopping the cycle of crazy that comes along with him.

Like a true gentleman, he paid for our meal, and though I was about to complain, I kept my mouth shut. He left a generous tip for the thirsty hostess, and we were on our way.

On the way to our apartment complex, I was quiet mainly because the hoe in me wanted to hop on this man quick, but I needed to be cool. It just finished raining a bit, so the streets were wet, and the temperature dropped. It was the perfect weather for cuddling, and I was in the mood for not being alone tonight.

Glancing over at him from the corner of my eye, he was slightly leaned back gripping the steering wheel with one hand and the other grazing his chin and appearing to be in deep thought. Extremely focused, I turned away and focused my attention out the window. The vibrating of my phone had managed to catch my attention, and Nomi's name popped up onto my screen as I answered.

"Hello."

"You up?"

"Yeah, I hadn't even made it home yet. I should've listened when you told me not to go out with that bitch. You need something out of the apartment?"

"Girl, Dri and I just got into it, so I'm not staying here. I was just calling to tell you I'd be home."

"You okay?"

"Yeah, nothing some wine can't handle. Where are you?"

"Um, headed home. I went to get food, and I should be there in a bit."

"Wait, with the fuck who?"

"Bye Nomi, I'll see you when I make it to the apartment."

Within minutes, we arrived at our apartment complex, St. Marais. Kenji opened the door for me, and I stepped out as he followed behind while he hit his keypad, and we arrived inside.

"I enjoyed spending time with you tonight."

"That's your way of saying we need to do this again?"

"You women with y'all reverse psychology ass shit," he smirked, sliding his hands into his pocket. "T'on think you can handle me, my love."

"What makes you so sure?"

Stepping onto the elevator, I started to experience that feeling again. The intense heat between my thighs became unbearable, and once those elevator doors closed, I went with my move. Pushing Kenji against the wall, I rubbed my hands onto his chest and crashed my lips onto his.

Hungrily his tongue delved into my mouth as he gripped my ass from behind and took immediate dominance. With his vice grip, he moved closer, and his piece pressed against my leg. Running my fingers through his locs, I sucked onto his bottom lip, and in one swift motion, he'd scooped me into his arms. Holding my ass in his hands, he pushed me up against the elevator wall and began kissing my neck. Gently sucking, his tongue soon trailed to my earlobe, bringing his lips right back to mine.

Once the elevator arrived at our floor, we wasted no time traveling to my apartment, which was across from his. Stumbling inside, I removed my jacket, and he'd scooped me up into his arms again. Taking things to the couch, everything moved so fast, and while hiking my dress up, he started to kiss the inside of my thigh. Inching closer and closer, he lowered me onto his face and began to feast.

Gasping and moaning, I was shocked at how quick things escalated, but I was in no way complaining at the way this man was pleasuring me. His tongue darted quick, and then he began to suck then lick between each fold as if his life depended on it. With his hands on my hips, I screamed out and tried to move away, but there was no use.

"What are we doing? Wait, this is too fast, this is too…" Unable to continue my sentence, I screamed so loud my voice had cracked. "Oh, don't stop!"

He wasn't much of a talker, but the way he was eating

my shit as if it were a pie, I see why the nigga wasn't saying a word.

"Billi, what the fuck are you doing!"

The pleasure soon turned into embarrassment as I turned to the door seeing Nomi standing with her mouth hanging wide open.

"Nomi, I...I didn't know you were—"

"Bitch, I just told you I was on the way, and you're on my new ass sectional! Who the fuck is this?"

"Billi's pussy monster," Kenji stated cockily, turning to me. "Yo, tell your girl to come back when I'm done and lemme finish eating on that shit 'til I make yo legs shake."

"You got five minutes!" Nomi fussed, turning to head back out the door. Shutting it with a slam, I sighed at looked at Kenji's fine ass and shook my head.

"The roommate?"

"Yeah, and I wish this night could continue, but...I really didn't expect it to go this far. I—"

Grabbing my chin, he pulled my face to his and crashed his lips onto mine. In a haze, I shut my ass up and wrapped my arms around his neck, while he delivered a slap to my ass.

"I'm right across the hall if you ever wanna finish that. A'ight?"

"Let me walk you out."

Things did go a little too far, but at the end of the day, we were both grown ass adults. Opening the door, an unfazed Nomi glared at him and rolled her eyes while barging inside.

"What's up with ya girl?"

"She's just Nomi. I'm used to it. I enjoyed you tonight, and I really appreciate everything. I needed this."

"Like I said, I'm right next door. I'ma let you go ahead

and handle that, but I'll see you when I'm hungry again. Cool?"

"Goodnight, Kenji."

"Night, ma."

Returning inside and locking up, I knew Nomi was about to let it fly. Soon as I walked into the kitchen, she started to shake her head.

"Billi, who the fuck is that?"

"His name is Kenji, and I met him tonight. Before you even start, I—"

"You had a nigga you just met tonight in our home with your fuckin' pussy in his mouth? Bitch, all I fuckin' know is he better have money or something because that's just some shit you don't do, not to mention you still fuckin' Joey!"

"Why are you judging me? For your information, I hadn't fucked Joey in months ever since I found out he was back at home with his wife so you can dead that. I'm single. What's so wrong with me finding somebody I like and being an adult."

"You meeting a nigga on the first night and having him eat you out is not you being an adult, Billi! Are you out of your damn mind? Is this some crisis type shit you going through? If it is, this is not the way you need to go about it."

"You're supposed to be my friend. Instead of downing me, could you at least be supportive of my decisions? I am a grown ass woman, and last time I checked, I'on fuck with my mother, so don't even try your luck with thinking you gonna talk to me any kind of way!"

"Fine, do what you want. However, since you're such a grown ass woman, you need to find out where you're staying next month because this lease is ending, and I'm not renewing it. It's time for you to take some responsibility and woman the fuck up, or this world is going to spit you the fuck out. Now you're my girl, and I love you, but Billi, you need a serious reality check because that what I just walked in and seen is not okay."

4

Kenji

"I started to think you wouldn't come," Ameera stated tearfully.

"I wouldn't miss this for the world. You know big bro got you, come here."

The rustling of the leaves and the soft whistling of the wind matched today's mood, especially with today marking one of the hardest days of my life. Christmas was days away, yet a few days before, we were hit with the heartbreaking news of our mother being no longer. Her death shook our entire world, and truthfully, it's been two whole years and neither one of us has been the same since she took her last breath.

"I miss her so damn much, Kenj. Why'd God have to take her away from us when we needed her the most?" Ameera questioned, sniffling. "We're so lost without her. The holidays aren't even the same without her. Daddy doesn't understand, but I don't think I'll ever be able to get over her being gone."

"I wish I had the answers for you. I really do, baby girl.

Unfortunately, we gotta keep going no matter how hard it hurts. We both know it's what mama would've wanted. I can't even begin to tell you how fucked up I am, but I have my moments, too. I want you to know we have each other, and that's all that matters."

While I remained emotion-free, this behavior was the norm for Ameera, and I couldn't even begin to understand how she'd felt being a motherless daughter. If I could take the pain away, Lord knows I'd do it in a heartbeat. Unfortunately, there was no such thing and as the big brother, I needed to hold her up at all times.

"I'm sorry I'm late, but I lost track of time."

Leave it up to Theo, also known as our estranged ass father, to ruin the mood. Before I even showed up here, I knew Ameera most likely asked him to tag along, but that didn't necessarily mean I had to be cordial with the nigga either.

"Thank you for coming, daddy."

"I told you I'd make a way." He half-smiled while pulling her into a hug.

It didn't take a rocket scientist to figure out that there was apparent tension between us. I was a very emotionless individual, but whenever I saw this bastard, it was almost as if I lost all of my common sense.

"Kenji," he greeted. "It's been a long time, son. You… seem to be doing pretty well."

"No need for the technicalities, pops. Just know I'm straight. Whether you agree with the way I'm living or not, I'm good."

"I never will understand the hatred you have in your heart towards me—"

"I'm not even about to do this right here at my mother's resting place, man. See, that's your problem. You're too busy worried about the wrong fuckin' thing."

"Kenji," Ameera fussed. "Not here! This is not about you or daddy. We're here for mama. That goes for both of you. No wonder she worried herself sick with wishing and hoping that maybe you two would reconcile! Mama is gone, yet you two still stand here and act like we have all the time in the world to right our wrongs."

"On that note, I'll come back on my own terms. Meera, I probably won't be at the crib when you get there, so you'll have to use your key."

Taking the higher road and choosing to walk away from the one thing that mentally fucked with me, it showed extreme growth.

Truthfully, I wasn't ready to accept or get past the issues shared between my father and me. As the only son, I was always protective of my mother, and from the moment I was old enough to know right from wrong, it was where I noticed pops wasn't as real as he made himself out to be.

Taking a detour, a drive around the city was just what I had needed. With the radio turned off, my thoughts were running rampant, and it was much better this way.

I'd lost respect for his ass a long time ago. It stemmed mainly from seeing how he treated my mother behind closed doors and when he thought I didn't notice. As a boy, I remember staying up many nights wiping away her tears or hiding alcohol from her because she'd stumbled upon a scandal involving Theo.

He played football throughout his life and even went pro, so he was living the high life with no care in the world, not even for his Lupus-ridden wife or his children. A man is supposed to be the provider of the family, and a marriage is about compromise, but Theo held none of those qualities. He shitted on her when she needed him most, and his colors soon started to rise to the surface whenever her health had begun to decline.

Just thinking back on all those times, it brought about nothing but anger. For years, it has always been millions of arguments and sometimes even physical, but now it's gotten to the point where I no longer respected the coward.

I'd driven around the city for so long that the sun disappeared, and instead of heading to the crib, I figured this would be the best time to blow some steam off at the gym. Pulling up within minutes, the parking lot was scarce and damned near empty, which was perfect. Grabbing my duffle bag and stepping out the whip, it chirped and locked as I stepped inside.

"Hey, handsome."

"What's good, Nina?"

"Nothing much," she flirted, batting her thick ass eyelashes. "The spot's been pretty lonely here without you. How you been?"

"I can't complain, love. Just taking it one day at a time."

I was an asshole, through and through, but respect went a long way. Not to sound like a cocky mothafucka, but I was used to women throwing themselves at me. Shit, I was a good looking ass nigga, and these women dropped like dominoes whenever I stepped in the room.

Nobody was currently on my radar, but Billi. She'd been on my mind from our first encounter. Usually, I was never the type to fuck around with a random bitch, but her persona was unlike any other woman I'd ever encountered. She was unusual from the type I'd go for, but there was something about her that I couldn't quite put my hand on.

Emerging from the locker room and plugging in my AirPods, Roddy Rich's "The Box" started to blast throughout my ears. Heading to the treadmill for a slight warm-up, I started to get in my zone and initially blocked out all things around me.

ABANDONMENT, along with feeling as if I were never good enough, were some of the things I'd battled whenever I was a child. Now being that I'm much older, I found it to be a struggle with opening up and allowing individuals to see me for my true self. At twenty-five years old, I should know better, be better, but honestly, I allowed my anger to take over way too much of the time.

Sometimes I wished we could reverse back the hands of time. As I sat staring at this picture of mama, the pain deep down in my heart would never be filled. As I tried my hardest not to shed a tear, commotion soon interrupted my precious moment, causing me to sigh. Judging by the time, Billi and this nigga were just getting started with the arguing. Fortunately for her, I was in the mood to start some shit, and this nigga had just given me the reason to do that.

Pulling on a sweatshirt, I opened the door and traveled across the hall. Beating against the door, the yelling ceased, and within seconds, the door swung open. Tears were streaming against Billi's face as she wiped them away.

"Yo, who's that at the fuckin' door? Bitch, I constantly tell you to shut the fuck up and keep these nosey ass mothafuckas outta my business, but you fuckin' hardheaded!"

"Is this nigga putting his hands on you?" I questioned.

Shaking her head, no, I noticed the bruises on her arm and started to see red. Pushing past her and entering the apartment, I was stunned to see that he was that rapper nigga that always stayed in the blogs. If I remember correctly, his ass was married, but he was causing a ruckus as if he owned shit.

Noticing the white residue around his nose, I had to laugh because these corny ass rapping niggas were all the same.

"Homie, you lost?" he asked, standing to his feet. "You fuckin' this nigga, Billi?"

"Nah, she ain't fuckin' me yet, nigga, but the way I had her moaning." I shrugged. "Best believe I'll be in that thang in no time. Oh yeah, by the time I'm done wit' yo coke headed ass, she'll have some new dick in her life. That's just the reality of it, brudda."

I was a shit talker. Those words set him off, and he took a chance with trying to tackle me. Due to my reflexes, I was much quicker and hemmed him up against the wall. It'd took everything in me to not fuck him up, but I knew I could potentially end this nigga's life with my hands.

"I'm doing you a mothafuckin' favor," I yelled through clenched teeth. "So, if you know like me, you might wanna fuck around and leave before I really fuck you up! If I hear bout you even much breathing the same air as her, nigga, your mother's gonna be planning your mothafuckin' funeral. You got me?"

"Billi, you gonna let this nigga talk to me like this?"

"Fuck that! Don't look at her, my nigga! You leaving or you want me to remove you myself?"

Shrugging my hands off him, he didn't say a word as he nodded and glanced at Billi. Making it easier for my ass not to murder him, he left and made sure to slam the door on his way out.

Appearing to be shaken up from whatever this nigga had done to her, she went to lock her door and proceed to pour herself a shot of Hennessy.

"Whoa, slow down. You'on need that shit," I spoke, snatching the bottle from her hands. "As long as I'm around, that nigga's not gonna fuck wit'chu no more, and I mean that. A'ight?"

Nodding, she wiped away her tears and took a deep breath. Pulling her into a hug, out the blue, she started to sob, and from that moment, I knew I needed to protect her at all costs.

5

Billi

TWO MONTHS LATER

"Look at my girl," Nomi smiled. "See, this is what I was saying those few months ago. Look at how you leveled up, friend. Just know that this is our year and I, for one, am so proud of this come-up. Check out this mothafuckin' glow, bitch!"

After the holidays, I just felt the need to level up and leave the bullshit in the past year. It took a while for me to realize that I needed to stop sitting around and sulking in my own damn misery. Unfortunately, it took me to hit rock bottom in order for my ass to soar. Now, it's a new year, and I'd successfully managed to move into a spacious condo, my nail business was soaring, and I was initially doing the damn thing.

Nomi may not have known this, but Joey and I have been in a toxic ass relationship from the moment I decided to jump my stupid ass on his dick. Even in the essence of knowing he was married with children, I still wanted to play the role of a bitch just wanting to fuck around with a nigga who had a bag.

Everything that glitters truly isn't gold, and I was

initially fucking the devil. With the glitz and glam that's attached to these types of niggas, they're just as fucked up as any other nigga off the street. Mentally, Joey was fucked-up, and for some odd reason, I loved that shit until it had gotten to the point where he'd become emotionally abusive, and it was just entirely too toxic. His love for cocaine was entirely too much for me, and it ignited the majority of our arguments. Thankfully, a certain someone entered my life and made me realize I was worth much more than I thought.

"So, are there any suitors to wine and dine my girl for Valentine's Day?"

"Like who? I'm too busy trying to chase this bag, girl. I'on have time to be entertaining no nigga."

"Don't try to act like I'on know you are fuckin' around with that nigga who you had eating you out on my good ass couch, bitch."

"I wouldn't say we were fuckin' around, but he's cool. I haven't fucked him if that's what you mean, but it is nice to have someone positive in my corner. I'm good on a lot of things this year. I was stupid enough to fuck around with a married man, and I don't wanna be that girl any longer."

"When's the last time you spoke to him?"

"Joey? Girl, ever since he called himself stepping to me at the apartment and Kenji overheard it."

"Ooh, okay, so your new man shut that shit down like a bad fuckin' song, huh?"

"He's not my fuckin' man. Calm down. Enough about me, are you ready for this wedding, big time?"

"I swear it seems like August is getting closer and mothafuckin' closer. I'm excited, but deep down, I'm just ready for everything to be over with. I'm already shacking the fuck up and much to the disapproval of his family, my own folks are not too sold or enthused on the fact that it's not being done the right way."

My phone started to ring with an incoming FaceTime call from Kenji before I could give my bout of advice. Trying my damn hardest not to blush, I went off for some privacy to answer. After accepting, his face soon came into view, and it looked as if he'd left a training session with Elon.

"You good? Looks like you've been working hard."

"You still out with your girl?"

"Yeah, we're just having lunch. I have one more last client for the end of the day, and then it's ten more tomorrow."

"Damn B, you doing fuckin' nails or selling work up in this bitch?"

"Ignorant ass, no it's just nails. Why what's up?"

"What that schedule looking like for next week?"

"Kenji, what the fuck you got up your sleeve nigga?"

"Just lemme know if you can be free next week for about three days. That's all." He smiled, licking his lips.

"I can be."

"A'ight that's all I need to know. Are you letting me stay the night tonight or what, Miss Funny Acting?"

"I guess so, Kenji. I'll see you later."

"Later, Boog," he spoke, using the little nickname he'd given me.

Returning to Nomi, she had her eyebrows raised, and I immediately started to laugh as she began to shake her head.

"What was all that about?"

"He was just checking in per usual."

"Checking in, huh?"

"Nomi, don't fuckin' start bitch."

Going the Distance for My Hitta

AFTER LUNCH WITH MY GIRL, it was back to the money. Ironically enough, my last client for the day just so happened to be Erial, when the last time I heard from this bitch was when she ditched my ass at the club.

I can admit to being a stupid, gullible ass bitch when it'd come down to forming new friendships, but with some of these hoes, they switched up so bad you never really knew who to trust. I had no issues with Erial. I was all for women getting their coin, but I wasn't about to be stupid either. I've been burned one too many times by going around and using the term friend loosely, but that'll never happen again. At the end of the day, it was all about business and fair enough, Erial played a huge part in bringing around new clientele when I needed it.

From the moment I'd decided on not attending college, back when I lived underneath the same roof as my mother, her only rule was that I couldn't be living in her house doing nothing. For a while, I was confused on my next move, but I'd managed to find my passion for doing nails. In the beginning, it started as a quick side hustle, but with mama's help, I was able to do nails for some of the most significant people in the industry.

Eventually, I worked my way up to becoming a traveling nail technician, and maybe sometime in the future, I'll be able to settle with getting my own location and hiring an entire team of my own. Nevertheless, for now, I had to work with what I was given.

Pulling up to Erial's house, I sent her a message saying I was outside while I started to gather my items. Arriving at her door, she stood with her teacup Chihuahua in her hands and a blunt between her lips.

"Long time no see, girl! How you been?"

"With the move and everything, I've been making it. Where you want me?"

"We can sit in the den or go upstairs, whichever is best for you. I can't believe it's been this long since I've seen you. You know we normally always quick to go to a party or any type of turn-up. It's nice to see you getting your shit together, girl."

"Yeah, but when it's time for priorities, it's time to buckle down, you know."

Erial was a get it out of the mud type of bitch. I didn't really know the details of what she did for a living, but the bitch was paid. She occasionally traveled from here in New Orleans to Atlanta or her place in California. We used to be much closer than how we are now, but personally, I felt as if certain things happened for a reason.

I was no hater, but I also was in no business of befriending someone who refused to be on this level-up train with me. Even as I sat here being as professional as can be, I could be tripping, but I could lowkey feel some sort of tension between us. Like a professional, I ignored it and kept it pushing.

"Thank you for coming on such short notice. I could only imagine how busy you've been lately."

"Ain't shit been popping this way and as long as you make an appointment, I'm able to make it do what it do."

"Girl I'm not even supposed to be in town, but I needed to come see my boo who I haven't seen in a while."

"Boo? Since when are you ever settling down for a nigga, Erial?"

"Before you even start, no, he isn't a dope boy. Well, I hope he isn't. You know how these niggas are, girl. I'm sure you and I both know how shiesty these men can be. Hopefully, I lucked up with this one."

"Sounds like you got a good one. Everybody ain't able, chile."

"I'on usually like to brag on a nigga, but girl, he is so mothafuckin' fine. He dicks me down so damn good." She sighed, shaking her head. "I'm getting fuckin' wet just thinking about his ass."

"Must be damn nice, and with the way you're talking, it sounds like you really like this nigga, huh?"

"Fuck that. He just doesn't know I'ma be the one to marry his ass. Wanna see a picture of him?"

"Girl, I'm not trying to be all in your business with your men."

"Oh, whatever, you know you're my girl."

Reaching for her phone, she went to her pictures, and literally, all the blood in my body started to boil. Playing the game, I talked my shit and gave her, her props but this was just why I watched who I called my friend.

Staring right at the picture of Kenji on her phone, something told me the certain surprise that he had up his sleeve would be no longer once I was finished with his ass.

I ONLY TRUSTED one person with my business, and that person was Nomi. With no other friends, I spent the majority of my time in my head and nine times out of ten, and the crazy bitch was dying to come out whenever a nigga had me fucked up.

Technically speaking, Kenji wasn't my dude. We weren't fucking around, and no stipulations were made for us to even agree to a situationship. All I knew was he sold dreams and sweet-talked his ass right into my life, and it was like a breath of fresh air. I needed some positivity, and for the first time in my life, it felt damn good coming from someone I was insanely attracted to.

Based on the stories he's told me, he wasn't emotionally or mentally wired for anything similar to a relationship. We bonded over our fucked-up situations, we flirted, and that was that. However, I'd be stupid to allow a man who was already involved with a bitch I'd known to think he could one up on me.

"B, come and open up the door!" Knocking like he was the damn police, I had just finished with the food. Answering the door and smelling as if he'd just gotten out of the shower, Kenji's cologne swirled in my nostrils as he pulled me into a hug. "Why you acting funny and shit?"

"We need to talk, so you might wanna sit down."

"Here you go with the bullshit." He sighed, plopping down onto my sectional. "What's the problem?"

"Do you know a girl named Erial?"

"Yeah, she's some bitch I used to fuck occasionally a few months back. You know I always told you whatever you gotta ask a nigga, just come straight out with it. So, what's the deal?"

"Well, the bitch is someone I'm familiar with. I did her nails today, and she happily says how she's in town to see her man in which she then proceeds to show me a picture of you. So, you tell me, what is the fuckin' deal, Kenji?"

"Who am I with damn near every night?"

"I—"

"And I asked you a question. Apparently, you're going by what these hoes saying and not the nigga you laid up with damn near every night. See, that's your problem. You're so fuckin' used to niggas doing you dirty when you'on even realize when a real one has your back, man. If all I wanted was pussy, trust and believe, I would have been got that up outta you."

"You need to start being honest with me, and that's just the reality."

"Be honest about what? I ain't fuck the bitch in months or any bitch for that matter. You really think I'm stupid enough to be lowkey pursuing you and supposedly fuckin' around with this random, irrelevant bitch?"

"Oh, so now you pursuing me?"

"Don't even do that. You know what you're doing, man. Chill."

"Fine."

6

Kenji

Waking up from a well-needed slumber after Billi did the damn thing in the kitchen, I was feeling like a new man. Checking my surroundings, her side of the bed was empty, but I could distinctly hear music coming from the front. The time on my phone read *7:07 p.m.*, which meant I'd been sleeping for hours and completely lost track of time.

"Well, well, well," Billi cheesed, turning down the music. "Looks like the dead has arisen. How'd you sleep, handsome?"

"What type of shit you put in that food?"

"You just needed a good ass meal. Damn, you never had anybody cook for you before?"

"To be honest, nah, I'on trust eating food from just everybody. I haven't had a nice home-cooked meal like that since my mother. My sister attempts, but it just doesn't hit like it's supposed to. Aye, we good?"

Pretending as if she didn't hear me, I did feel guilty. I haven't fucked Erial since that night I met Billi. Truthfully, I didn't know what this girl was doing to me within the span of knowing her for a few months, but somehow, she damn near made me want to be a better version of myself.

"Is that your way of asking me, do I trust you?"

"Potentially."

"I don't mean to get too sentimental, but we're both grown, Kenji." Billi shrugged. "We're both grown, and we're adults at the end of the day, so whatever happens, you're gonna need to allow it to happen," she started.

"You're here damn near every night. I cook for you, mind you, I don't just cook for any nigga. I enjoy having you around, and I'm pretty damn well sure that you feel the same way. What are you so fuckin' afraid of?"

"I'm wired differently, and that's the God honest truth, but you're different as well, and it's something about you that I can't begin to put my hands on. I guess all I'm saying is…I'on wanna fuck you up, B."

"You're talking in circles." She sighed, pushing me onto the couch.

Climbing into my lap, Billi took my face into her small hands and smiled a bit, in an attempt to search my face for some sort of further explanation.

"How about this?" She suggested. "We're both in no shape for anything serious. I dead ass just love being around you because you're like a breath of fresh air. I say, we take it slow and see where things could go."

"Only under one condition."

"Which is?"

"I just want you to be well aware of what you're getting yourself into. I'm fucked-up and all over the place, literally. I caught a glimpse with what you went through with dude, and I'm not trying to do that to you, I—"

"Shut up and just go with it, nigga. Besides, I ain't even gave you the pussy yet, and you've come much closer than half of the niggas I've been with."

"Half? Well, fuck, how many it's been before me!" Her face turned into a scowl, causing me to laugh as she smacked her lips. "I'm fuckin' with you, but about what I had to tell you. I hollered at Elon, and I accepted a gig out in Houston, so I was wondering if you wanted to join me."

"You playing games?"

"No, I'm dead serious. This the first time I'm doing something like this so, pardon me for sounding comical."

"All this time you've been fighting, and you've never brought a girl with you?"

"I usually don't allow myself to get in too deep with females nowadays," I admitted. "Look, fuck all'at. You coming or not?"

"Ask me nicely."

"B."

"Don't be rude, be a gentleman," she cheesed, wrapping her arms around my neck. "I mean, you might as well. Then maybe, I may…possibly agree to your invitation."

There it was. Once I'd gotten a taste of that paradise between her thighs, it was over with. Here she was, currently swooning me, and I couldn't even try to pretend like the shit wasn't working. Her gorgeous ass had me under her spell, and I hadn't even dropped dick yet.

Those luscious lips and the way her natural face, completely free of that harsh makeup, glowed flawlessly. Her dark brown eyes low and focused on me while I wrapped my hands around her waist.

"Billi, will you please do me the honor of joining me in Houston?"

"That's more like it. I'd be more than happy to."

"EASY, SLOW IT DOWN," Elon coached. "There you go. That's it. One more round, let's get it!"

Next week's fight in Houston will be the first of the year since taking a small hiatus for the holidays. Though I could be quite cocky, I felt like nobody was fucking with me. Fighting was indeed a physical sport, and it was best to always use your mind, first and foremost. This fight was essential because it would be my first of the year, plus I'd have Billi in the stands, so I had to play it smart. I lived and breathed this shit, mainly because it was all I had to express myself. Nobody in my family understood what it meant to freely be able to do what I wanted without any judgment.

I sometimes would like to think it's the main reason why pops and I tend to clash. He's upset at the fact that I didn't follow his footsteps with football, and in his eyes, I'm living wrongly. I chose not to engage in any conversations with an individual who isn't supportive. That pretty much sums up the relationship we have. He stays in his lane, and I remain in mine. It's as simple as that.

"You performed well today. Are you ready to take on this character? I hear they've been talking big shit on this match."

"I'm not with all the talk. I'll do my talking in the ring. I see it. So many bitches and niggas from the hood send me that shit, but you know that don't do anything to me."

"I trained you, champ, trust me, I know. So, about this young gal?"

"What about her, OG?"

"It's gotta be serious. Shit, I never see your black ass with anybody."

"You know I'm private as hell, but she's cool. We've been getting really close since December, so I figure if she can put up with my ways, she's good in my book."

"What's her name?"

"Billi."

Elon's expression of approval soon faded once he turned his attention towards the entrance. Following his gaze, Erial had entered the building, and of course, Elon dipped because he wasn't too fond of her.

Her presence right at the moment was irritating as fuck, but that's the thing with crazy bitches, you could never be too careful. I should've known as soon as I fucked her in the parking lot, she would be on the nut shit once again.

"I knew I'd find you here."

"Where else would I fuckin' be, smart ass?"

"Be grateful," she spoke, playfully rolling her eyes. "I hear you're going to Houston for a big fight. Damn, where's my invite?"

"I ain't send one."

"You really get on my damn nerves acting like that, and why the hell you ain't been responding to my texts?"

"Erial, you acting so new to this shit when you know how I am. The last time we even fucked around was in December. I never called or texted you before, so what makes you think I'ma start now? Chill out with all that extra ass shit, man."

"You must got a new bitch or something?"

Twisting her neck, the attitude was apparent, but I was in a pretty good ass mood today, so I refused to have her rain on my parade. Then again, fuck it, I owed this bitch no loyalty.

"I fucked you in the parking lot of a mothafuckin' club on my damn birthday. Just because I dropped dick on you, don't mean you my bitch, and I'm pissed off because you acting like you'on know that. You always with this tit for tat as if I owe you something. Fuck that."

"So that's how you really fuckin' feel? All this time, I've been looking stupid, thinking this was going somewhere, and all I am is a piece of ass to you!"

"You said the shit, not me."

After those final words, I disappeared to the back and left her ass looking stupid. When you assume, you tend to make an ass out of yourself, and right now, she was looking like the biggest ass. I usually call myself holding off on being mean, but nowadays, you couldn't help but to keep it real.

Today's session with Elon was much needed, but after weeks and days of prepping for this fight, I needed to drop by Apollo since we hadn't seen each other in a minute. My homie was the average day hustler, so you never really knew the type of shit he was on, and surprisingly, today, he was chilling at the crib.

"I'll be mothafuckin' gah damn, the champ done decided to fuckin' bless a nigga with his presence and shit!"

In typical ass Apollo fashion, he was surrounded in a room full of half-naked bitches, some weed, and his most well-trusted workers. He loved this shit. I had to be honest, he was living the high life, and as long as my brother was happy, that was all that mattered.

"Can I get you a drink, baby?" one of the women purred.

"Rubi, give him some space, bitch!"

"Nah, I'm good. I appreciate it, though." Taking a seat, we did the signature handshake we've been having since we were kids as I shook my head. "Working hard or hardly working, nigga?"

"Always working, brudda," he stated proudly, flashing his diamond grill. "Me and the dudes are holding it down for you at home. This is the big one, huh?"

"I done handled bigger opponents, so this is fuckin'

slight work. I know Elon and me are gonna bring it on home, but nigga, since we here, lemme tell you about this bitch Erial."

"That girl knows she's too damn fine to be that fuckin' crazy. Is she still on that shit?"

"Nigga, when is she not on that shit?" Shaking my head, he passed the blunt as I declined. "She called herself pulling up at the gym, dawg. Before I knew it, I set that hoe straight."

"All that time pops tried to shield yo ass from the hood and look at it coming up outta you! I'm proud, my nigga, really and truly, but I heard she done got some niggas fucked-up, so be careful."

"I should be telling yo ass the same fuckin' thing, bitch. All these women you got in this hoe!"

"You can never have too much pussy," he cheesed. "I'm in heaven, and I guarantee you, I'ma sample every single one of them, tonight."

"You won't be satisfied 'til that lil' ass dick falls straight the fuck off."

"Boy, fuck you. With all that shit you talking, you better leave that fight with not a single scratch or bruise. Man, when you gonna stop this underground shit and get signed and do this shit for real?"

"Signed enough for somebody to call themselves owning me? Fuck that shit."

"I'm saying tho. Imagine being professionally recognized for knocking niggas out on a daily, man? You could be the next Mayweather!"

"I'm trying to be better than anybody to ever do this shit, especially coming up outta New Orleans. If the opportunity presents itself, then maybe I may have a change of heart, but for now, I'm content where I'm at."

7

Billi

Having settled in Houston for about a day, Kenji spent the mornings and half of the day prepping for his fight while the plan would be to spend our nights together. The trip itself was supposed to be for a few days, but he took it upon himself to have us stay for a week, which I saw no problem with.

Right about now, instead of painting the city, we decided to keep it cool for the night and chill. He was laid on his back, and I found comfort on his chest with a blanket covering us while we watched cartoons, our current being a favorite of mine, *Meet the Robinsons*. For a nigga who boxed for a living, he seemed pretty interested to the point where he didn't want me talking or uttering a single word. I expected him to fall asleep, but it had his full attention.

"Where you going?" He frowned at my attempt to get up. "You're supposed to be watching this shit with me."

"I've seen it before, Kenji, and relax, I'm just going to warm up my wings."

"Just hold off. I wanna see how it ends."

Rolling my eyes, he pressed play and rested his hands

on my ass while we continued to watch the remainder of the movie. About twenty minutes later, the ending credits began to show, and I was shocked to not hear a smart remark from him.

"Well?"

"Why them people always gotta make shit so sentimental?" he fussed. "Since when they started doing that?"

"This movie is pretty old, and I guess they wanted to shed light on the adoption process for older kids. Did you like it?"

"It kinda hit home for me."

The distinct change in his tone proved that he was most likely alluding to something serious. We have been getting to know each other for a little over three months now, but he wasn't too reluctant on opening up, and I refused to get him to do something he didn't feel comfortable doing.

"You okay?"

"I was adopted when I was two years old, B," he admitted. "I was one of the lucky ones to find my forever home with people who didn't care whether I biologically belonged to someone else."

"Do you remember anything about your birth parents?"

"Not really. I think maybe the trauma from whatever happened to me in my childhood has caused my mind to block it out mentally. But after losing my mom, it's like I shutdown. The only person I really talk to is my sister, Ameera. My pops and I have been bumping heads for a long time now, and there ain't no coming back from it."

"Is that the reason why you fight?" I asked. "To potentially deal with everything you've been through?"

"Yeah, most def. When I fight, it's like I'm battling everything and everyone against me. It serves as a coping mechanism after losing my mother and the bullshit with my father. It's not the best way to relinquish any emotion, but it works for me." Kenji stated, focusing his attention on me. "Lemme guess, I scared you off now, huh?"

"Not at all, your flaws are what make you unique, and I'm not judging you. You know you can trust me, right?"

Kenji started to turn away until I grabbed his chin and forced him to look at me. For the first time, I realized I finally stumbled upon someone who was far more emotionally damaged than me.

"Kenji, you can trust me, but I can't make you do anything you're not ready for."

"I hear you, and I want you to really hear me when I say this, but…I'm trying. I'ma get there, but it's gonna take some time."

"I can respect that, and we can go as slow as you need."

Catching me off guard, he leaned forward and pressed his lips to mine. Just like the first time we'd kissed, my body reacted immediately, and, in that moment, I wanted all of him. Gripping my ass aggressively, I could feel the largeness of his dick pressing against my inner thigh. I wanted him terribly, and I knew he felt the same way, but clouding this moment with sex wasn't the best decision in this situation.

"Stop," I playfully fussed. Ignoring me, Kenji continued to slap my ass and entice me. "I tell you what. You win this fight, and I give you all the ass you want. How does that sound?"

"I'm getting ass, regardless! Fuck that."

"Oh, you just know you are, huh?"

"Yeah, because I'm like that."

"Alright, YB, whatever you say."

DUE TO THIS fight being underground, the environment was completely different from what I'd expected, but none of it mattered because all I was focused on was Kenji. Chilling in the back until showtime, his trainer went over the game plan for the night and watching him in his essence. It just turned me on.

Judging by the expression on his face, he was in complete game mode. Not wanting to interrupt his groove, I stayed in the corner glued to my phone with occasionally stealing glances at the masterpiece of the man standing a few feet away from me.

After what seemed like an eternity, Elon disappeared off. Kenji bounced around as the adrenaline continued to run through him. Turning to look at me, we met each other halfway as he sat down and pulled me close to him. Sighing, I had to admit I was nervous, but something in me just knew he was going to perform well.

"Kenji, they're ready for you!"

Standing to his feet, we shared a kiss and made our way out to the ring. Trailing behind, I found a spot to stand close to where I could catch everything. The crowd was immaculate, and the noise was intimidating. His opponent looked to be ready to get the ball rolling, but Kenji could handle that immediately.

The time had finally come, and the fight started. Watching Kenji deliver and take everything his opponent attempted fired off something within me. After the fourth round, I was yelling like a mad woman and had fit right in with the rest of everyone watching. His opponent's eyes were on the verge of closing, and Kenji himself had a little bruising above his eye, but other than that, he was physically okay.

Going the Distance for My Hitta

At the start of the fifth round, the opponent had something to prove. Delivering blow after blow to Kenji's side, in an attempt to try to damage his ribs, they were pinned in the corner.

Working his way out, Kenji clapped back with a few jabs, causing the dude to stumble back and delivering a blow to his jaw, he'd fallen down.

"Yess!" I screamed. "Baby, that's what the fuck I'm talking about!"

The crowd initiated a countdown, but before they could reach ten, he managed to stand back on his feet.

"Fuck him up, Kenji!"

Noticing that he started to clutch his side, I was on edge, but I hoped I was wrong. Blow after blow, Kenji came out like a machine that was stopping no time soon. Pinning him in the corner, the opponent hung onto the ropes. The two squared up once more. Kenji dodged another punch, doubling back with two of his own that connected perfectly. Aiming for his side again, the opponent landed successfully.

The sound of the bell erupted, signaling the end of another round. Running over to the corner, I didn't like the look I saw on Kenji's face.

"I'm good!" Kenji shouted. "Lemme go ahead and body this nigga!"

"You better do just that too. We worked too hard on this!" Elon added. "Take him on out like I know you can, son. You hear me!"

At the start of the round, Kenji made sure to do just what he said he was going to do. Both of them were doing the damn thing, but initially, Kenji was working smarter and not harder while his opponent was performing a bit foolishly.

I could see the exhaustion all over his face as Kenji

delivered each time effortlessly. With a successful combination of something I've never even seen before, it'd knocked the opponent off his feet, and the crowd went crazy. Screaming excitedly, I was so proud to be able to witness him compete and come out a winner.

Little did I know, tonight's celebration would come to a halt due to Kenji having bruised ribs and having to receive stitches due to the wound above his eye. Luckily, these crooks had an underground doctor on call, and he was able to assert the injuries without us having to visit the hospital.

"Ahh, fuck!" he shouted as the doctor pressed down on his ribs. "You think you pressed down on that shit hard enough, doc!"

"Your ribs are bruised for sure, but thankfully, you have no fractures or broken bones. I say he should rest up before the next match and he should be good to go with some—"

"I'm not popping no pain pills. I can handle it."

"Suit yourself. Well, my work here is done. Congratulations on your performance tonight, and you all have a nice night."

Leaving, Elon also went out to take a call, giving us some time alone. Walking into Kenji's space, he pulled to him with a cheesy smile as we shared a kiss.

"I'm proud of you. You did so good. I hate you're hurting, though. You gonna be okay?"

"Ain't nothing I can't handle, Boog. Thank you for coming to support me. I appreciate you. I'ma just have to take a raincheck on killing that pussy tonight, tho."

"Why you gotta be so trifling?"

"Because you like that shit."

Interrupting our moment, the door opened, revealing this nigga who looked like he was no stranger to the streets accompanied by Elon and another stranger. Giving them their space, Kenji securely held my waist as I started to feel this uncomfortable vibe.

"Here are your earnings, big dawg. Five stacks off the rip," he spoke in his raspy voice. "I also got somebody here who's been wanting to meet you. K, this is London. He trains professionally around these parts and has been watching you for a minute now."

"London Gaines," the stranger announced. "You're way too talented to have your talents shielded underground. The professional boxing world has been waiting for a fresh face such as yours. How long you been at it, young buck?"

"About twelve years, and I appreciate the gesture, but I'm uninterested in whatever you're offering. Now, if you'll excuse me, I got somewhere to be."

8

Kenji

Joining Elon for breakfast the morning after a successful fight was our go-to routine. Over the past few years, we've been a duo. I couldn't even try to front like I wasn't sore as fuck right now, but it's the price you have to pay for being the best of the best to ever do it.

"First and foremost, let's have a toast to another well-deserved win. You did a good job, champ."

"I couldn't have done it without your teachings, OG. You know anything about this London Gaines cat?"

"His great grandfather and I used to run in the same circle back in the day, so we're quite familiar with each other. His boxing career was an interesting one, but he took the professional route. After his last and final win, London announced he wanted to try his luck with training and has been doing so ever since. All the boxers he's represented have held record-breaking titles, and their career stats are some of the best I've seen since my start."

"He's real big time, huh?"

"If you've done your research like I constantly tell you to, then you'd know he was serious about his offer. You take up these fights and bring in about five thousand or a solid ten depending on your performance. Imagine how good it'll feel to earn double that amount. The game of underground boxing is as dangerous as it is tricky."

"The last thing I need is spotlight when I know I'm good at what I do. It's the same shit Theo tried to get me to do, but I turned him down. I need all these folks to know I'm more than just Theo Breaux's son. I'm my own man at the end of the day."

"I just want what's best for you, son, but honestly, this vendetta you have against your father is going to do nothing except lead you to a pit of despair. You're much smarter than this anger trying to consume you."

"What you suggest I do?"

"The decision is all yours, Kenj, but the offer won't remain on the table forever."

I strongly disliked being compared to my father, especially when I've worked so hard to get away from his spotlight. Another thing that tended to grind my gears was damn near everybody in my circle trying their damn hardest to get me to bow down, mainly when I've been spoken on not being down with the shits.

AFTER A MORNING well spent with Elon, I joined him in an Uber on his way to the airport. Returning to the suite, judging by the cleanliness and organization, Billi was wide awake. Entering the bedroom, her flawlessness radiated as I stood at the doorway just mesmerized by how naturally she looked in this element. She only sported a robe, which hung loosely at her shoulders and her hair in a messy bun while she ran her mouth on that damn phone.

"Lemme call you back, girl. He just walked in, so I need to start getting ready."

"I wasn't trying to interrupt."

"You weren't?" She smiled, walking into my arms. Standing on her tiptoes, we shared a kiss, and she pecked them again.

I had a point to prove, and before Billi could wiggle out of my arms, I gave her that look while taking my time to open her robe. Scooping her up into my arms, we soon moved over to the bed.

The sexual tension between us intensified the moment she began removing my shirt. Pushing Billi up against the wall, my lips went towards her neck, causing a sexy moan to escape from her lips. Cupping her ass in my hands, I laid back onto the bed as her hands grazed my dick through my sweats.

Slapping her ass once and grasping it, she started to wince. Taking matters into her own hands, her soft hands rubbed my chest as she planted kisses along my abs. Her hands then reached into my sweats, stroking my growing erection in her hands. Pulling them down, she started to lick the tip and put her mouth to work. Taken by surprise, seduction loomed in Billi's eyes while she kept her eyes on me.

Within seconds, her skills had gone from nice to immaculate, and damned near had me speaking gibberish. Coming up to take a breath, I took this as the opportunity to flip her onto her back. Helping me out of my sweats, Billi started to laugh and bite her lip. My hands soon found their way between her thighs, and I dipped my fingers inside her wetness. Bending down to plant kisses between her inner thighs, her scent caused my mouth to water just like the first time.

Carefully licking between her folds, I darted towards

her clit and took my time. Pulling her closer to my mouth, her hands got lost within my locs. Moaning out and throwing her head back, her chest heaved up and down, followed by the curling of her toes. Sucking gently and taking my thumb I rubbed at her clitoris to the point where she couldn't even handle it as her body began to buck.

Forcefully grabbing my face and pulling it to hers, our lips moved undeniably. Grabbing onto her thigh, damn near in a trance, I positioned myself into Billi's opening. Searching her eyes for some sort of approval, Billi nodded with her lips lingered against mine and gasped lowly.

The warmth of the treasure between her thighs greeted my shaft like paradise. Creating a pleasure-filled ride, I was all in and proving my point. Holding onto the headboard, she held my face and squirmed underneath with her face scrunching into these indescribable expressions, which made my dick rock hard. Overpowering me and pulling my hair, she got on top and slid down onto my shaft so effortlessly.

Slowly rolling her hips in a back-and-forth motion, Billi soon arched her back as our lips connected. Kissing sloppily, her tongue danced in my mouth, and I palmed her ass with a well-needed vice grip. She playfully bit down onto my bottom lip, holding onto the headboard. Clenching down onto my dick with a vice grip of her own, her moans erupted throughout the room as her voice cracked. Instead of hopping off, she stayed on top, and without warning, my seed exploded in her.

Taking things up a notch, she positioned herself down on all fours with the perfect arch. Turning around, her eyes were filled with lust, almost as if she was feening for me just as bad as I wanted her.

Sliding in once more, Billi matched my rhythm, but once I started the deep strokes, she could no longer hold on. Her juices coated me and began to seep onto the sheets as I plunged deeper, hitting her G-spot. Perfecting that arch, she gripped the sheets and started to scream my name.

"Uh, uh," I fussed. "Don't fuckin' run!"

Pulling her hair, she started to fuck back against me as the powerful sound of our skin slapping against one another accompanied her moans, followed by my grunts. Breathing quietly, she looked back at me with a devilish grin and started to slow down, her muscles once again clenching down on me. In an instant, I attempted to pull out, but it was useless resulting in her laughing.

"Pussy was too good, huh, baby?"

"You talking shit? You must be trying to go all damn day, huh?"

"Maybe I am."

HOUSTON HAD BEEN A WELL-NEEDED vibe for both of us. Sadly, our trip would be coming to an end once we boarded our flight back to Louisiana first thing in the morning, but I needed to get one thing out of the way before we left for good.

"This is our penthouse and the largest unit we have. The individual who resided here traveled a lot, so the place still looks good as new. Some recent renovations were also completed for more space to those who are looking to expand families or settle into something before finding an official home. You say you're an athlete?"

"In a way, yeah, I am."

"Well, Mr. Breaux, I'll give you and your spouse a moment to browse. I'll be out taking a work call."

After giving it some thought over the past few days,

Going the Distance for My Hitta

along with doing my research, I managed to do some digging into London's background. From what I found, he was pretty much the big leagues. He broke records and had a lot of recognition under his belt for being well known in the professional boxing world, so I decided to have a meeting with him.

I've been looking to relocate from New Orleans for a while now, and Houston was beautiful, so doing a little house hunting for the moment seemed like the proper thing to do. Taking Billi along for the ride was in my best interest as well, although jumping to a whole new state would be irrational since we both were still on the need to know basis.

"What you think?"

"This is way too big for just one person, Kenj. It is beautiful, but why exactly are we looking at this penthouse?"

"I took the meeting with London," I stated, grabbing her hands. "Besides, I've been looking to move outta the city for a minute. I guess all I needed was the extra push."

"Move?" She frowned, her facial expression changing dramatically. "I'm all for you doing what you love, but... you know what? Never mind."

"Hold up. What's the problem?"

"Nothing, um, I need some fresh air."

FOR THE REMAINDER of the day, Billi was distant. I asked her to accompany me to the meeting with London, but she was giving off the attitude that she didn't want to be bothered, so I gave her the space she needed.

Staying true to my schedule, I arrived at London's gym right on time. Stepping inside, judging by the interior of this gym, he was the showoff type. Hell, if I had the same stats as him, I'd probably be doing the same, but my mother always warned me to steer clear of showoffs.

"Kenji Breaux!" Dressed in designer from head to toe, London met me halfway as we shook hands. "I wanna thank you for taking me up on my offer, my brother. Follow me."

Numerous accolades, belts, and photos from throughout London's career were plastered all over the walls. There were two massive rings on each end of the gym, while in the far corner, there was exercise equipment along with all types of training items.

Following London into his office, I took a seat, and he shut the door behind us.

"Elon has spoken very highly of you, and though you are underground, I've been keeping up with you. You're extremely talented. You're about two hundred and something pounds, right?"

"Two hundred fifteen."

"I'ma keep it real with you, youngin'," he announced. "Nobody's really checking for an illegal nigga out here, risking his life to make some stacks. With the professional aspect, everything is in your hands — your earnings, your way, and everybody you allow on your crew follows your lead. That goes for your trainers, med staff, photographers, sports agencies, and the list goes on and on."

"Apparently you were checking for me. You're talking a real big game, so what you get outta this?"

"Just an opportunity to mold you into becoming a legend. The offer is yours if you want it."

9

Billi

"Be sure to inform your clients before you take a weeklong ass vacation. You know damn well you can't leave one of your most loyal customers hanging like that!"

Getting back to the money after Houston was the best coping mechanism, especially since my mind kept thinking about Kenji. Things had turned sour between us, and it's been extremely awkward and confusing judging by neither one of us making the first move to mend things.

Right now, Diamond, a loyal client of mine, had been cracking jokes all damn day. Thankfully, she was my last client, but she was also a damn good friend as well. She currently resided in Alabama with her husband and their two children, but she frequently traveled, due to her career as a female barber. She was mainly booked by entertainers wanting their cuts blessed by Diamond, and let's just say my girl was making her way in the world.

"You know whenever you need a re-up, I got you. How are the babies?"

"The youngest is so spoiled, girl. I blame her daddy. My big boy is growing so much before my eyes. Seeing them grow every day is making me wanna consider having a third one, but girl, Zyair is not having it."

"That's code for I'm still planning on putting it on him so I can get my third."

"I'on know how you know it. Speaking of, what's going on in your love life? You're always tight-lipped, so I know it gots to be a brother worth hiding, huh?"

"I dropped the last and started conversing with this guy. In my old building, he stayed right next door and literally came to my rescue when the other dude was going crazy one night. We've been inseparable ever since. He is actually the reason why I was out of town, but we semi got into an argument, and we're not speaking right now."

"Your luck with these men, Billi, I swear it's always something. Judging by how you sound, I can tell you must like him. What's holding you back?"

"I do like him, but he's been through some shit, and it's fucked him up. We're still on the get to know each other basis, but we practically do everything couples do. He doesn't like titles, but he tends to confuse the fuck outta me, sometimes." I sighed. "We had sex for the first time and bitch when I tell you this nigga's dick is gold…I think that's partially the reason why I'm so pissed that I ain't heard from his ass."

"Okay, back up because it takes hell and high water for me to get you to talk about a nigga, let alone brag about him? Oh shit, this gotta be serious. Aww, look at my little baby, she's catching feelings!"

"Stop," I whined. "I hate feeling like this because I get to overreacting, and I do stupid shit. You know how I am."

"You gotta get out of that habit of thinking everyone you come across is gonna use you up, Billi. Ever since I first met you, you've always had this guard up, and that's okay, but sometimes baby girl, you gotta let that guard down."

I rarely ever allowed myself to open up to people, but those who did have the opportunity of knowing the real me would say I struggled with self-acceptance and yearning for a love like no other. For years, I spent my earlier years going through niggas who weren't worth my time or patience. Some of them would be attached to females, but even with knowing that, I continued to pursue them. Initially, I used them to try to mask these feelings, but in the end, I only felt worse.

Taking things this far with Kenji and actually seeing that he was different from most was like a literal breath of fresh air. I've never had a man so adamant about pursuing me, although he too battled with his own demons. He expressed his troubles and some events of his past, which actually shows that he's actually trying to become a better him. That alone spoke volumes, but I feared that he feared of getting himself hurt in the process.

"You think I should be the bigger person and call him?"

"I say you should. If the week you spent in Houston was as enjoyable as you claim, then I know you're missing him terribly. Right after I leave here, please give him a call and be the bigger person."

As I considered Diamond's words, I cleaned up my workstation and retired to my bedroom. Allowing Tory Lanez's crooning to soothe me, I picked up my phone, and before I could even dial his number, my doorbell had started to go off.

Running my fingers through my fresh silk press, I slid my feet into my house slippers and went to answer the door, only to reveal Kenji. Stepping to the side, I allowed him inside, and he entered.

"I know it's been a few days, but I needed to talk to you

because I'm confused about why you are giving me the cold shoulder."

"You can't even own the fuck up, can you?"

"You gonna keep being childish and shit, or are you gonna let me fuckin' talk?" Kenji's tone was demanding, but he kept his cool.

Rolling my eyes, I folded my arms across my chest and waited for him to continue.

"Look, I told you from the jump I was no good with shit like this, but that ain't no excuse," he started. "I can't help if I do certain shit and it pisses you off, because just like you'on know what ticks me off, I don't know what ticks you off either. Before meeting you, I had already made plans to move, and honestly, it's all just bad timing."

"Let's not forget you pursued me. I didn't ask you to come into my life and make me want you. I was doing bad without you! Now, as soon as you get what you want, you dipping, right?"

"Billi, you're not hearing me!"

"Then what the fuck are you saying! Was I not supposed to catch feelings?" I questioned, standing in front of him. "Fuck that, because you know I'm not the only one. If that were the case, then you wouldn't even be here right now!"

"I wish I can make you understand, I really fuckin' do. This right here, I'on ever do this shit for no bitch! I'on wanna hurt you, Boog. You special to me, and I tend to fuck over the main people who mean the world to me. I can't be that for you right now, I—"

"You're not the only one who has fuckin' trust issues, Kenji! I've been used, abused, and talked about by niggas who claim they'd never hurt me and look at what it's done to me. However, unlike you, I'm woman enough to stand here and admit that something deep down within me sparks when I'm with you. I've longed for that for so long, and now you're telling me just to ignore it."

"What point of me saying I can't be that for you, don't you fuckin' get?" Kenji shouted.

"Well, do me a favor and stay the fuck outta my mothafuckin' life!" I screamed. "But don't fix your lips to say shit to me when you see a nigga treating me the way I deserve to be treated."

Storming over to the door, I opened it and waited for him to leave, but he stood there fuming. Not moving a muscle, his face was emotionless, but it's what frightened me because, with Kenji's unstable ass, you never knew what the outcome would be.

Making his way over to me, he slammed the door and picked me up while crashing his lips onto mine hungrily. Placing me onto the island, he grabbed my throat erotically in a way that immediately made me wet. His lips lingered against mine, and I reached up to remove his hands. Opening his mouth to speak, I stopped him and pecked his lips once more.

"If this is gonna be a thing, and then you'll need to trust me, Kenj."

This journey wouldn't be an easy one, but if he allowed it, I was all in. Nodding softly, he pressed his forehead to mine and soon placed his head into the nape of my neck. On that day, I vowed to show him my true self and never look back with hopes of him doing the same.

"LORD, I still can't believe my best friend is in a stress-free ass relationship. All I know is this nigga better like my food or we gonna have some problems. Are you excited about tonight?"

"He just a health nut at times, but he'll be okay." I cheesed, nudging her. "You ever thought we'd be doing this?"

"Hell the fuck no because your ass is known for picking horrible ass men, but judging from what you tell me, this Kenji is something. By the way, I'm still not too keen that this nigga was eating you out on my fuckin' sectional."

"You're never gonna let me forget that shit are you, bitch?"

"As long as I'm still living and breathing, you're gonna forever hear about it."

Nomi and Yadriel were due to wed sometime in August. With time steadily winding down until the big day, we often squeezed in girl time aside from our hectic ass schedules. Tonight was super special because she was hosting a little dinner at her home, which would be where I introduced Kenji officially as my man.

I had to do a lot of begging and pleading to get the nigga to crack, but he agreed, and here we were. Typically, he wasn't too keen on meeting new people, but this might be the start of a bond between him and Yadriel as well. I was confident that he'd be respectful and all the things that made me enjoy him, but I hoped and prayed this dinner would be anything less than awkward.

"Alright, girl, lemme go get him, and we'll be back."

"Okay, be careful."

Arriving at his building in no less than ten minutes, I started to blow his phone up mainly because he was taking his sweet ass time. Powering my car off, I stepped out of my car and figured he was most likely moving like an old ass man. Stepping onto the elevator, I pressed the number to his floor and tried his phone again, only for it to continue ringing.

The elevator dinged, signaling that I'd arrived on his

floor as I slid my phone into the back pocket of my jeans. Completely forgetting that I'd left my spare to his door in the car, I banged on the door crazily as it swung open, revealing a female.

"Damn, who?" The girl appeared just as stunned as me. "Who are you?"

"Who's that at the door, Ameera?"

"I'm K's sister, Ameera. You must be the infamous Billi?"

"Yeah."

"Come on in. He's been locked in that room all damn afternoon."

Entering, I traveled to Kenji's bedroom, where the door was closed. Opening without warning, I walked into what looked like a tornado with clothes and shoes all over the damn place.

"Kenji, come on before we're late! Where you at?"

"Damn, Boog, gimme a mothafuckin' minute to wash my ass!"

"You're just now showering? I fuckin' told you I was gonna be here at six," I fussed, entering the bathroom.

Pulling the shower door open, once I caught a glimpse of this huge bruise placed on his face accompanied by a cut on his lip, I voiced, "Are you serious? What the hell happened to your face?"

"Ouch, fuck!" He winced, wiggling out of my grasp. "I got a lil' carried away at my session today. Now, are you gonna get the fuck back and let me shower or what?"

"Ten fuckin' minutes is all I'm giving you."

"A'ight, damn!"

10

Kenji

It didn't take too much to tell that we were far away from the hood judging by this gated ass community. It wasn't as if I wasn't used to shit like this, but Billi didn't even give my ass a heads up on what I was walking into.

"The fuck this nigga do for a living?" I questioned, observing our surroundings. "Move work?"

"Don't be ignorant, push the doorbell."

I had a bad habit of speaking first without taking into consideration how others would perceive my delivery. Not only was this a big ass night for Billi, but I also had to show these friends of hers that I wasn't like any of the other niggas she'd ever been with.

Her friend had already had a bad perception of me since she had walked in on my devouring Billi, but let's hope it was left in the past. I would sure hate to have to get ignorant, but I assured Billi I would be on my best behavior.

The door opened, revealing Nomi. I was good with faces and the scowl on hers damn near made me laugh out loud. I guess Billi must've given her a look because the scowl turned into a fake ass smile within seconds.

"Y'all are just in time. Come on in and make yourselves comfortable."

Similar to a mansion, the grandiose interior design reminded me of my childhood home, which was the same size as this. Since Nomi soon-to-be husband was the provider, I knew he had to be one of those pussy-whipped ass types to do whatever for his bitch. I just prayed for his sake that he was no corny nigga because then this night would be awkward as fuck.

"Dri, come here!" Nomi shouted, rolling her eyes. Following the sound of her voice, he emerged from the afar, and from the moment he walked in, I could tell he was no stranger to the streets.

"What's up, man?" he greeted respectfully, shaking my hands. "Welcome to the humble abode. It's about time you invited somebody to the crib, Billi!"

"Nigga, shut up. Guys, meet Kenji, and Kenji meet Dri and Nomi."

"We've met," Nomi announced. "It wasn't quite the first impression, but…it's in the past."

"Y'all, let's just go and eat."

Once a few drinks were thrown into the mix along with the food Nomi prepared, we were all conversing as if we'd known each other for years. I wasn't too iffy on getting to know Nomi because off the rip, she seemed judgmental and the type of friend to micromanage. According to Billi, she is like a sister to her, and the reason why she's such a bitch is that she's overprotective.

Despite our first encounter, I was given the chance to see a completely different side of her. From what I've seen, she and Dri was a powerful pair. Before tonight, I would've pegged Nomi as the loud-mouthed controlling type, but she really was just rough around the edges. Once I learned she was originally from Pigeon Town, it all started to make sense.

Overall, the dinner went well. Giving the ladies their space, I followed Dri so that we could talk man to man without commentary from the women.

"I appreciate your hospitality, man. You and your lady are living it up. Billi tells me the wedding in August. I'ma be honest wit'chu, marriage scares the shit outta me, big dawg. I commend you."

"No lie, I was used to fuckin' around and not too much looking for anything special. Once I met Nomi, it's like she made me wanna become a better version of me. I was on the wrong path, getting ready to follow in my father's footsteps and shit. She entered my life, and from the moment we met, she straight out was like she's not with the hood shit. I respected her for that, and she gave me a run for my mothafuckin' money. I was jumping through hoops and shit, trying to impress her ass!"

"No wonder her and B such good ass friends," I admitted, shaking my head, causing Dri to laugh.

"I can only imagine the type of shit B be on. When I first met Nomi, she couldn't stand my ass. However, them girls been through a lot of shit, so I couldn't blame either one of them for thinking what they thought about me."

"I can admit to being fucked up because I'm still dealing with some shit I don't wanna face right now. I got B in my corner wanting me to be open and all this, but I can barely get her to open up to me."

"I'm sure you know she doesn't have a relationship with her mother. Her pops have been locked up for years, and she barely knows him. I never saw her in no serious ass relationships or no shit like that, but…I can't judge her."

"I try not to be too in her business and shit, but the more I break away at her, I see these insecurities, and it's a shock to me because I'on even allow shit to get this far. This the first time I ever allowed my guards down on behalf of a woman."

"We're one in the fuckin' same, bruh, real talk. I used to call myself fuckin' around on some slick shit. I'll never forget I had this lil' hoe I was keeping on the side, the moment Nomi caught a whiff of that shit." Dri sighed, shaking his head. "That was all she fuckin' wrote, my G."

"Nigga, no lie, you got my ass scared and shit. I know B got it in her to fuck some shit up. How you knew Nomi was the one to the point of marriage?"

"I put her through some shit, no lie. I was fucked up to a point of no return, and not once did she give up on me. Not saying us as men should ever put the women we love through any of that bullshit, but she took the time with making sure I was good, mentally, and emotionally no matter how much I'd hurt her. Time after time, I took her for granted until I realized, this woman really loves my stupid ass.

We'd broken up, and one day I saw her with some other dude, and a nigga I got so fuckin' mad. Here I'd done my dirt and just the sight of seeing her with somebody who wasn't me fucked me up. It made me wanna be better for her and be this man she needed me to be, and from the moment I got down on one knee, I vowed never ever to put her through that shit."

With sitting down and getting to know Dri, it didn't take much to tell that we were damn near one and the same. It's very seldom I cross paths with niggas who think the way I do or tend to make the same dumb ass decisions I make. You could barely cross paths with real niggas nowadays, so this seemed like the beginning of a budding friendship if I said so myself.

━━

TORY LANEZ FEATURING Chris Brown's "The Take" erupted from the soundbar across the room as Billi's small hands roamed over my shoulders, massaging away the tension in my muscles and ultimately ending the night on a good note.

We've spent so much damn time together that it felt crazy whenever I woke and not having her on the other side of the bed, but I couldn't dare bring myself to expressing that to her, at least not right now.

"You and Dri seemed to hit it off really well. Did you enjoy yourself?"

"Yeah, he a cool ass dude. I ain't gonna lie. I thought he was corny as shit, but we chopped it up on some real shit. It was well needed. Your friend still ain't letting go of that night, I see."

"Well that's Nomi, take it or leave it."

"Dri told me something tonight."

"And what was that?"

"Something about never seeing you in a serious relationship. What's up with that?"

Stopping altogether, I felt her getting up, and before I could turn over, I noticed her making her way towards the bathroom. Hopping up out of bed and catching her before she made her exit, I grabbed her arm while noticing her avoiding eye contact.

"I ain't mean to step outta bounds, but don't run away from me. Why you running? I'm right here, Boog."

"Promise you won't judge me," she said in a voice barely above a whisper.

Going the Distance for My Hitta

"Never that. Come on and talk to me."

Making our way over to the bed, I pulled her into my lap and observed her.

"Um, my first love was someone I met a little after I graduated high school. We grew up together, and I just was never good enough for him. I foolishly allowed him to use me in the hopes that maybe I'd finally be good enough for him to take me seriously. To make a long story short, he broke my fuckin' heart. From that moment, I felt nothing for the longest. I'd pursue guys who were in relationships and shit because I didn't want that feeling of things getting too deep, and I'm disappointed.

All of that changed when I met Joey. In the beginning, he was what I thought I'd needed. His drug abuse was unlike anything I've ever dealt with, but for his sake, I stayed even with knowing he was married with children. Part of me enjoyed the fact that I have always been a side bitch because I felt like it was what I deserved. For some reason, I believed it was all I was good for because, in the back of my mind, I always was thinking that it'd be another situation like with my first love."

The dying moment I have been waiting for was finally taking place. It meant the world to me seeing Billi in this purest form because I knew it'd taken her a while to get to that point. I had some skeletons of my own, but for women, they chose not to elaborate on certain shit.

"I'ma keep it real, I have no right to judge you for what went on in the past. I'm the future, and we gonna leave that bullshit in the past. Fuck them niggas along with that shit they put you through. I'll never do that to you. You do know that, right?"

"Usually, when I open up to niggas, they tend to run away from me."

"I'm not just any nigga, sweetheart. I'm a grown ass

man who doesn't mind fixing what another stupid nigga fucked up."

"Can I ask you something?"

"Shoot."

"Who hurt you?"

"Ya know, nobody's ever asked me that before. I'on wanna make this about me, I—"

"K," she pleaded in a soft tone. "I wanna know these things about you, but that can't happen if you don't meet me halfway."

I didn't want to admit it, but this woman was definitely getting me intact with the side I tend to shield from everyone else. The only other woman who had known all of me was my mother, and there hadn't been anybody else since. My heart was cold, and it'd take hell and high waters to get me to break, but Billi was damn near closer than half of these lowdown bitches I called myself fucking with.

"My birth parents, first and foremost." I nodded. "Over the years, I guess I can say my pops. I expected a lot from him as a kid, and I was let down countless times. Over time it turned me the way I am now, and I never wanted to give my heart to a woman because I have real bad abandonment issues. Every person who enters my life, I feel like they'll leave."

The way Billi's eyes stared into mine, it sparked something within me. I always spoke on never being the type of nigga to open up or potentially put myself in a position solely based on seeing how certain situations and things changed people. I'll be the first to admit to not wanting to ever lose focus on my hopes and dreams.

As crazy as it sounded, I was willing to go that extra mile or do whatever was needed to build a foundation of trust with this woman sitting before me.

Her lips began to form into a slight smile while she

took my face into her small hands and pressed her forehead to mine.

"I really just wanna get to know the man beyond this wall you have built up. All the pain and hurt you've gone through, I just wish I could take it all away and see you flourish into this strong, admirable man that I know you are. I'm here for you…for as long as you'll allow me to be."

11

Billi

I had spent the majority of my life worrying about what others had thought of me. I wasted my time with niggas who didn't even deserve half of me, better yet of all of me. I'd run through has been ass niggas, niggas who'd broken promises to me, and niggas who saw it fit to use me up until I was basically nothing. Out of all of my years of living, I'd never met a nigga to express his truest form until I'd crossed paths with Kenji Breaux.

Gradually we'd both broken down barriers within ourselves and opened up to one another. I had a broken man on my hands, but I couldn't even do the most because I, myself, had suffered from my fair share of doubts when it came down to men. The first man to ever break my heart was my father, and ever since then, I made a vow to myself to never allow another man into my heart. For some odd reason, with Kenji, I felt comfortable knowing he wasn't like most I'd been with.

I guess it was safe to say that we'd both found common ground with having gone through the people who are supposed to love you the most, initially giving up on you.

Going the Distance for My Hitta

Kenji doesn't like to admit it, but I can see through his pain, and I see a man just sorely wanting to be accepted, loved on, and appreciated. I was no different. In this world, the only person I could trust was myself. Of course, I had my girls, but neither one of them could seem to understand why I was truly wired this way.

Often times, this would cause me to put the blame all on my mother for never really being around when I needed her most. She foolishly allowed her wealth to raise her only child to where I turned out to be a fucked-up product. In her mind, moving me away from New Orleans would serve her right with keeping her baby girl from not being fucked-up, but it had done nothing except hurt me in the long run.

Basking in silence, the only noise that could be heard was that coming from the soundbar. Kenji's favorite artist, Rod Wave, erupted throughout my space as I attempted to work some magic on this head of his.

Dipping my fingers in a concoction of shea butter, coconut oil, and jojoba oil, I applied it to his loc and twisted while placing a clip onto it. I carried on this routine up until I finished re-twisting his entire head and then proceeded to style his freshly twisted locs into rope twists, or two stranded twists as some would call them.

"You real quiet back there. You better not be fuckin' my shit up, Boog."

I dead ass hated the nickname Boog because it reminded me of booger. I call myself telling his ass that each time it escaped from his mouth, but the way it rolled off his tongue just gave me chills.

He claims his reason behind it is because before Nipsey Hussle passed away, he admired the way he treated his woman, Lauren London. In his eyes, I was his Boog. I hated the shit with the greatest passion, but he ate it up.

"You gonna fuck around and make me punch you dead in your shit. I was thinking, so thank you for being rude with interrupting my ass."

"Thinking about what?"

"You."

Anticipating his response, before I could finish up with what I was doing, he turned around to face me. I noticed this specific look in his eyes that I'd rarely even saw, but I knew it caught him off guard.

"Us."

"I do something wrong?"

"No babe, you did nothing wrong. I tend to get in these moods sometimes. It's not your fault."

"You know I'm here if you wanna talk."

"Not now. I'll be good, but let's just get into making you look fine as fuck. Okay?"

"A'ight. I'on need you getting all fuckin' sappy on a nigga."

This nigga's arrogance would cause any bitch to turn their nose up in an instant. He honestly didn't mean any harm, though. His rude ass was just set in his ways with talking any kind of way and getting away with it — one of the things that irked my nerves, yet it made me fall harder for him.

"Can I be real with you?"

"I'm always listening. You know that. What's going on?"

"I've been talking to E about potentially making the switch to the pro level. I dead ass didn't wanna tell you a thing until it was legit, but I got a meeting first thing in the morning."

"What's stopping you?"

"Ain't shit stopping me. I just don't have a want for a nigga trying to make a buck off my name because of what

I do. The whole point behind me staying underground is because I get to do my own shit the way I wanna do it with no rules. Think about it, B. If I take a deal with somebody wanting to manage me, I'm doing shit their way and not mine."

"In life, you have to make sacrifices, baby. That's just how this life works. Either option you choose, I'll support you just as much as I have been doing. I feel like he does have a point, though. There's a lot of good money in the pro boxing world, and you're damn good."

"You saying I should?"

"I'm saying you should consider it and do what you feel is best."

I took pride in uplifting my man and doing whatever was needed to make him feel like the best man he could ever become. I understood he had his issues, and he was damaged, but it's honestly what made me want to keep him close to me at all costs.

The way this world took pride in downing the black man is not the type of shit I was on. Whenever the time was right for me to have children, I'd be sure to instill within my baby boy's mind that he is a black man, and though this world tends to hate his entirety, I will protect him at all costs.

"You like it?" Admiring the finished product, he flexed in the mirror with an enormous ass smile on his face.

Turning around and placing me on top of the sink, I giggled as he pressed his lips to mine aggressively. Hungrily he pulled me into him and put his forehead to mine with that smile of his I'd started to adore.

"Down boy," I whispered, grabbing his hands. "We need to slow down on the fuckin', and that's me being dead honest with you. As much as I enjoy your dick, I need you to be mindful that we're playing with fire, and neither one of us is ready for a kid right now."

"I know how to control myself. What that mean?"

"You've nut in me damn near every single time we've had sex, Kenji. Stop lying to yourself. I know I got good pussy, but like I said, we need to be more careful."

"So, you giving my ass blue balls? All you gotta do is bend over!"

"Don't be an ass!" I fussed, jumping down from the sink. "I mean it. Either we cool off, or you wrap it up."

Returning to the bedroom, I crawled into bed and grabbed my phone. Shocked, I stared at the missed call, stunned that my mother had the audacity to hit me up. We haven't spoken or exchanged words since last year, so she had to have something up her sleeve seeing as though she'd hit me up.

"I'on feel like cooking. You want me to go pick up some food, or we using Uber Eats?"

Vibrating in my hand, the same number was plastered onto my screen. Staring at it, I started to answer, but once Kenji entered the room, I declined it.

"You ain't hear me?"

"Um, I'm not hungry."

"You a mothafuckin' lie because if I get something, you not about to be prying in my shit. So I'ma ask you again what you want. I'm heading out now."

"Whatever you get, just get me the same thing."

"You straight? You look shook."

"I'm fine. Just hurry back."

━━━

"SO, THIS IS REALLY YOUR CAREER?" Ameera questioned.

"Pretty much. Eventually, I'd like to get a shop of my own, but that requires money I don't have right now, so yeah. Don't be like me. Please stay in school, get your degree, and boss up. I should've done the same, but I wasn't thinking."

Ameera was the complete opposite of Kenji to say they were brother and sister. Unlike him, she was a social butterfly and such an optimist. We rarely spoke because she's been so busy in school, but luckily, she'd prospered academically and was now on her break until the fall semester.

She'd been staying at Kenji's apartment, mainly because she didn't want to move with their dad and be lonely. For a girl her age, she was independent and had shit going for herself. With an older brother like Kenji, I highly doubt she ever had time to do what she truly wanted. Nevertheless, young ladies like Ameera were determined to make their mark in the world, and I admired her.

"He's changed for the better since you two have gotten together. I haven't seen him in such a light like this since our mother passed."

"I try my best, but girl, your brother is a handful. I just take my time with him. The last thing he needs is someone beating him down mentally and emotionally. He works my last nerve, but I appreciate him."

"He cares for you a lot. I know his weird ass may not like to admit it, but you're doing something good to him, and I'm all for it. He's different from a lot of dudes, but with you, it's like you don't even see the difference."

"I was taught to never judge a book by its cover, no matter what you see on the outside. There's always something great underneath the surface. Alright, girl, lemme apply some cuticle oil and you're all done."

The door burst open and in walked Kenji with food

just as he promised. I hadn't seen him since this morning when he left for training. Like the good girlfriend that I am, I figured it would be good to spend time with the girl to keep from her being locked up in this apartment all day.

"I got the goods for my two favorite ladies!" He smiled, kissing the side of my head. "Aye, Boog, I'ma be out late tonight. That's cool?"

"Out late doing what exactly?"

"Come on, I'ma be a good nigga."

"That's not exactly answering my question, K."

"And I, oop," Ameera commented. "Lemme see my way on out before this gets heated. Thanks for the Manchu, bro."

Taking a chicken wing from my plate, he went to sit at the table, and I placed myself on his lap.

"You really gonna embarrass me in front of my sister like that?"

"Stop with the theatrics and cut the shit," I joked, playfully hitting his arm. "Apollo?"

"It's my dawg's birthday, and he wanted me to come through. If you want, you can come with me."

"The last thing I want is to be in a room full of drug dealers. It's fine, but I just want you to be careful. Okay?"

"I got'chu," he stated, grabbing my chin. "What you and Ameera talked about today?"

"None of your business. After I eat, I'ma probably go nap in your room, so be quiet when you come in. Thank you for the food."

12

Kenji

"Can I get you anything, baby?"

"Sweetheart, if you know what's good for you, you'd back up. I hear his lady is crazier than a muhfucka!" Apollo warned. "We wouldn't need the big homie getting in over his head with the misses."

"Good looking out, big dawg."

Surrounded by some old and new faces, everyone in his circle saw it fit to come together with a small gathering for Apollo's wild ass. We'd been family for years now, so I had known practically everyone he'd come in contact with. Though I didn't trust some of these niggas, I always kept my mouth closed because maybe he saw something in them that I didn't.

"Yo, K, you still on that boxing tip?"

"You already know. My lady's in my ear about going pro, so it may be an option, too."

"Them damn women know they got a way of making you do certain shit, huh bruh?"

"Shid, I ain't complaining. Last time I checked, Tek I

thought you were on the road to getting married, my dawg?"

"Man, fuck that bitch! Aye, word to the wise, don't trust these hoes."

"Y'all niggas better not let Tek ass talk y'all into some bullshit," Lando added. "We've been boys for years, and this bitch is always in some shit with a broad. He can't get right!"

"Can't get right this fuckin' dick, nigga! I just don't trust these bitches. Apollo, nigga, you get in on this too?"

"I'm single, so I fuck who I choose." Apollo shrugged. "I'on love these hoes. I'on even know what the fuck got into K's love-drunk ass, but the nigga's been in a good ass mood lately, so lemme stop talking my shit."

"Y'all niggas always wanna talk shit when a nigga got his shit together. It ain't even all'at serious, bruh. I was feeling her, so I acted on that shit. We got a good thing going on, and ironically, I enjoy having her fine ass around. So, hell yeah, nigga, call my ass pussy-whipped all y'all want, but nothing beats coming home from a long ass day and having a good ass woman waiting on you. Fuck what y'all niggas talking bout."

"No disrespect to your lady, bro, but this bitch has to be top notch to swindle yo cold-hearted ass!" Tek explained.

"I told y'all this nigga was in love, dawg," Lando laughed. "I told y'all niggas."

I was used to these niggas cracking jokes and shit, but words didn't do a damn thing to me. If anything, it made me better. Plus, I never took anything seriously when it came down to these three.

While they were getting fucked up with bitches, pills, and liquor, I kept it cool with a few shots trying not to get too fucked up. Apollo's ass just had to have strippers at the crib, and as soon as the bitch started to give me a lap dance, my phone started to go off with an incoming FaceTime call from Billi.

Before I could answer, my phone had fallen out of my hands while another stripper had climbed on me. These aggressive bitches were fine as fuck, but my bitch was even badder to the point where these hoes weren't hitting on shit.

⸻

TIME STARTED TO FLY, and before I knew it, it was two in the damn morning. Thankful to have caught an Uber here, I began to look for one to go home just when things were starting to die down. I was tipsy, but I knew better than to call Billi, especially since I didn't answer her FaceTime from earlier. My phone was cracked, I was horny, and I just wanted to get to the crib, take a shower, and aggravate my bitch. My best option was to call Ameera.

"You do know it's two in the damn morning?" she answered groggily.

"I'm trying to get an Uber, and I can't find one, so come get me. My keys are in my room. I'm trying to keep from calling B."

"Alright, just send me your location, and I'll be on my way."

⸻

EVEN AFTER A LONG night with the guys, I somehow always stayed waking up at the ass crack of dawn looking for something to do. To keep from disturbing Billi's rest, I figured my best bet would be to go sweat out the alcohol in hopes that I would feel much better since I worked out regularly.

Arriving at the gym, once Elon caught a look at me, I knew it was going to be pure torture. Due to my clean eating, my choice to not smoke, or drink alcohol, I was classified as a lightweight. Best believe this old ass bastard took it upon himself to make sure I never stepped out of line with overdrinking or getting too hype with the nightlife. Workout after workout, drill after drill, I started to sweat bullets off the rip.

Yelling out on my second rip of sled pulls, once Elon clapped his hand and started barking, I had to switch to the battle ropes.

"I bet your hardheaded ass gonna think twice about going out when you know you need to be prepping! Hop back on that sled!"

I should have known he wouldn't take it easy on my ass, but this was the price you had to pay when you wanted to be a great. Completely disregarding his orders, I went off to the side and started to feel sick to the point where I began uncontrollably throwing up. I'd couldn't even hold it together while Elon stood laughing like somebody told the funniest joke.

"You gonna mess around and kill that boy, Lonnie!"

"His ass needs to be on the brink of death for being stupid," he fussed, throwing me a towel. "Clean yourself up and make yourself presentable. When you're done come to my office, I'd like for you to meet someone."

Shooting him a death glare, his business partner and old friend, Jacen, had come to my aid. Wiping my mouth, he shook his head and had to let out a laugh.

"Fuck you do to piss him off, young buck?"

"Nothing at all, your boy is just a hater."

Once I'd successfully cleaned myself up and was hydrated, I met Elon in his office only to see a very familiar guest seated. As if I already weren't feeling like shit, this was just what I needed, a surprise visit from this judgmental fuck.

"Son." With a fake smile plastered onto his face, I eyed him and kept it moving. "It's been a long time since we've last spoken."

"The fuck he doing here, man?" I questioned, turning to Elon.

"At the end of the day, I'm still your damn father, whether you like it or not, Kenji. Elon, would you mind giving us some time alone?"

"Take as much time as you need."

Leaving us to our privacy, once Elon dipped, I was extremely overwhelmed with anger, especially since I hadn't seen or heard from this man in months.

"I see you still disobeying my rules like you've always been doing."

"I ain't no lil' ass boy no more, that's for damn sho," I commented. "Never did obey you, and I won't start today. What you want, man? I got shit to do."

"Well, you ain't been doing shit. I'm shocked that your disrespectful ass ain't gotten locked up with this stupid decision to fuck up your life by fighting illegally. Your mother would be—"

"Don't you fuckin' dare. Nigga, the last thing that should be coming outta your mouth is shit pertaining to my mother! You think because you were the provider, we were supposed to bow down to you? Fuck that! I'll be damned before I respect a mothafucka who couldn't even be there for his family, but was quick to fall in the first piece of white pussy he—"

Hemming me up by my collar, I stared into his eyes and saw nothing but a coward ass man hiding behind his wealth. I refused to even flinch because this old bastard wasn't even worth my time or patience.

"Get yo mothafuckin' hands off me!" I warned, pushing him. "Look at you. Can't even do shit because you know the shit true. You a sad ass nigga, dawg, and I promise you that'll be the last time you ever disrespect me!"

Ignoring Elon as he called my name, right about now, I wasn't trying to hear any bullshit. He'd double-crossed me by even agreeing to allow my ain't shit ass father to even step in the same building as me.

"Kenji!"

"Nah, man, take yo hands off me! You supposed to be in my fuckin' corner at all times, so how the fuck are you gonna invite that nigga down to the spot and not even inform me, Elon? That's some fake ass shit, dawg and I'm not fuckin' with it."

"That nigga is your father, son! Calm down and just come back inside."

"Nah, I'm good."

This is exactly why I struggled with trusting certain people. Elon has been the only father figure I've had since I stopped believing in my own father. I guess, deep down, I never felt like I was a son of his. Even after we were adopted, I somehow always felt like the black sheep.

In the beginning, it was all happiness and him eager to finally have a son of his own. The minute I started thinking on my own and being able to see people for who they truly are, something within him just didn't seem right. I disliked the way he treated my mother, even throughout her harsh times with her sickness, and I damn sure didn't appreciate how his family always came second to his career.

Contrary to how I was currently feeling, once I pulled up into Billi's building, I was so pissed off that I couldn't bring myself to stop shaking. Grabbing my things and entering the building, I felt some sort of comfort knowing no matter how I was feeling or what I was going through, as long as I had my Boog, I'd be straight.

Using my key to walk in, she was chopping it up with her girls, and all talking had ceased once I'd stepped in. Not even bothering to speak, I disappeared off to the bedroom and slammed the door behind me.

"Y'all I'ma be right back. Something's not right with him." Opening the door, she was about to open her mouth and start fussing until she'd seen my face.

"Baby, are you okay? You can talk to me. Tell me what's wrong."

Shaking my head, she started to frown and touch my face with a sigh. Pulling her by the waist, I rested my head on her stomach and just closed my eyes, embracing her for the moment.

"Okay, okay. Um, everything's going to be okay. Just let me tell the girls—"

"No," I protested. "Just stay with me, Boog. Please."

"Okay, I'm not going anywhere."

13

Billi

"Are you sure you're up for this fight tonight, Kenji?"

Choosing to face his problems through fighting, I didn't know how to feel about tonight, specifically since Kenji's clouded his emotions with workouts and shutting the world out. It's only been a few days since his abrupt coming to my place. Although he no longer showed signs of irritation or discomfort, I just knew something wasn't right.

Refusing to answer my question, he simply kissed my lips, and that was basically telling me to drop it because there would be no discussing anything until he was ready to express himself. Not wanting to pry or pester, I left him to it and went to take my place outside, awaiting the fight. For support, I invited Dri and Nomi. This wasn't either one of their scenes, but for some reason, I couldn't be here by myself tonight.

The crowd was a bit on the rowdy side tonight, but it was all because Kenji would be facing an opponent from Michigan who had supposedly been wanting Kenji's head since previously losing to him sometime last year.

I'd been doing my research with this underground boxing world, and it was basically an anything says and goes fight. With Kenji going through whatever was bothering him, I feared tonight would have an unlikely outcome.

"Hey," Nomi called, rubbing my shoulders. "Aww, lemme find out you're nervous for your man tonight."

"I'on know about tonight," I admitted. "I just have this feeling he's not all the way there right now."

"My homie's got it," Dri added. "Relax and take a load off, B. He'll do good."

Trying to make myself believe those words were true, I just couldn't shake this gut feeling. I felt as if Kenji were going into this thing blind, especially with the weight of his problems on his shoulders.

All of those worries soon disappeared once Kenji stepped out, earning an uproar of cheers from the crowd. His opponent, on the other hand, wasn't like too much by the crowd, and they made sure to let him know how much they disliked his ass. Looking at the smile on Kenji's face, he basically ate the shit up and allowed it to boost him.

Once the fight started, I was anxiously on edge. The other guy was good and was putting Kenji to work. On both sides, both were performing up to par.

"Don't let him fuck over you, babe!" I screamed. "Play it smart!"

His opponent fired back with a blow to the jaw, causing him to stumble and lose his footing. While he was down, the opponent delivered multiple blows to his stomach, causing Kenji to fall and clutch his side.

Gasping, my heart dropped into the pit of my stomach, but Kenji managed to get back up onto his feet. The two went tit for tat continuously, and although he was barely standing, Kenji managed to dodge and jab him quickly before the round ended.

As the cut man tended to his wounds, I could tell that something was wrong. Rushing over to the scene, he and Elon were having a heated exchange.

"What's going on?"

"He's showing signs of broken ribs, and I'm trying to tell his dumb ass that he needs to call this fight!"

"I'm not calling no fuckin' fight!" Kenji growled.

"His eye is closed up, and judging by these wounds, he'll need more stitches," the cut man announced. "If he takes one more blow to this region, he'll be out for way much longer than he anticipated. Kenji, it's your call."

"I can beat this nigga, I'm not calling it," he repeated, shaking his head. "Fuck that. I won't!"

One of the things I strongly disliked about Kenji was the way he felt he often had to prove himself, especially when he didn't have to prove shit to anybody. As a supportive girlfriend to a determined, stupid nigga, I sat there and watched him partake in the worst thing ever.

Going into this round, he'd lost before he even had the chance to try to defeat him. Each effort Kenji attempted went a long way, but nothing could stop this man from coming harder at him each second. By the time the round ended, and Kenji was bleeding uncontrollably. His eye was closed and swollen, yet he was still refusing to call the fight.

The next round started, and once again, Kenji lost his footing after a blow to the face. He fired back with a few jabs of his own, but the opponent revved back with his fist and delivered an earth-shattering blow to Kenji's jaw, ultimately knocking him to the ground.

Mentally blocking out all noise, the only thing on my mind was rushing to his side, and once I caught a glimpse of him not moving, I didn't care who was holding me back. Fighting them off, Dri and Nomi rushed to my side to where I looked, seeing Kenji unconscious and laying there completely immobile.

THANKFULLY, the morphine was doing the trick to where Kenji couldn't feel a thing. According to the doctor, he had a ruptured kidney, a mild concussion, and a few broken ribs. Due to the wounds, he had to receive stitches, but luckily no drastic surgeries. If I could take all the pain away from him, I would, but since that wasn't likely, I just sat here at his side, waiting for him to wake up.

The road to recovery started once he was discharged from the hospital, but his mental just wasn't there. Each day passed, and he'd become a complete recluse, relying loosely on the meds to ease both the physical and emotional pain. He refused to go to his apartment, he didn't want to be bothered with the likes of his father or his sister, and he damn sure was barely putting up with my ass because we rarely even spoke.

"You gonna keep walking around here like I'on exist?" Breaking the undeniable tension between us, I didn't even expect him to speak up since he's been in his own world lately.

"I don't know how to talk to you, Kenji," I admitted, turning to him. "Ever since this fight, you haven't been yourself. I don't wanna do or say anything to piss you off, so I've been giving you your space."

"If you want me gone, then just say the word, Boog."

"Why do you always push me away when all I'm trying to do is be there for you?"

"Because I'on need nobody fuckin' feeling sorry for me!"

"Feeling sorry for you?" I repeated, stepping closer to him. "Whatever it is that's got you so fucked up, I'ma need you to take a step back and look in the mirror real fuckin' hard! All I've ever done is try to love you, Kenji, even when God only knows how frightened that shit makes me when I give my heart to a man! I walk on eggshells trying not to say anything that'll tick you off, I try to do everything I can to please you and this the thanks I get?

You spend so much time trying to push me away, that you'on even know how hard it is for me to see you like this right now. But fuck it! If you want me gone, then man the fuck up and say it. Say it!"

Standing up to him, my adrenaline pumped, and even with my expressing myself, Kenji still just stared at me stupidly. He couldn't say a word because I know I wasn't tripping with knowing that I wasn't the only one feeling this way.

"I can't make you understand it, Boog," he said softly. "I'on know why I'm like this. I'on know why I'm so fuckin' angry all the time, but what I do know is that I need you. Even when I'on wanna admit how much you've changed me, you have. I'm on track to becoming a better man because of you, and I know I might make it hard and shit, but I need you to work with me! Please."

Coming from him, I knew this took a lot out of him, especially since he never really showed any emotion whatsoever. I didn't even know why I was standing in front of this man crying, but these tears were showing the true emotional bitch in me.

There was something deep down within me that knew I couldn't just turn a blind eye to disregarding his feelings. The frightened part of me wanted to walk away, but the stronger side of me wanted just to love on him and give him everything he needed emotionally and mentally.

"I can't try if you don't allow me, Kenji. I can't constantly be shut out just because you're on this fuck the world shit. I can't be your emotional punching bag when you've had a bad day," I stated. "So, if you're willing to change these ways for me…then this can be smooth sailing from here on out."

Still not uttering a single word, he took his time walking over to me and wiping away my tears. Grabbing my chin, he brought his lips down to mine as we kissed sensually and completely started to forget about the world around us. His lips lingered against mine as he stared down at me intently, sighing in deep.

"Don't agree to this if you're not up for it, K."

"I'm all in, and I got you. You just gotta trust me."

"Do you trust me?"

"I do."

⊏⊐

RIGHT AFTER KENJI was given the okay to take it easy, he'd started rehab, and right after I would finish with my clients, I would be at his side every step of the way. This soon started to become a routine, and like clockwork, I was asked the unthinkable.

"Are you fuckin' outta your mind?" I laughed. "Baby, I—"

"Fuck all'at, lemme take care of you." Kenji smiled, caressing my cheeks. "You can still do your thing with your nail tech shit and I'ma get myself right. However, I can't start this journey if I'on have you by my side, which is why I want us to find a spot together and move into our own … just me and you."

"Who are you, and what have you done with my man?"

"Say you will?" he begged, pecking my lips. "Come on and rock with me!"

"Okay, alright! Fuck it, let's do it."

14

Kenji

"You sure do know how to make your lady happy, man. I'on even know her like that, but she's been smiling since we started moving shit in the crib. You'on think it's gonna get lonely for y'all in this big ass house, brudda?"

"Nah, it's perfect, and shit, I'm willing to do whatever I need to keep that smile on her face. Now that I do got you here, I just wanna thank you for the extra hand when I needed you, man. Shit has been real slow for my ass since I've been getting back straight."

"We family, nigga," Apollo nodded, dapping my hands off. "I just wanna see you level-up, no matter what the hustle is. Are you hanging up the gloves?"

"Not necessarily, I just hadn't been in the right mindset to start back fighting. I just got the green light to start back with my regular workout routine and shit, so I'm just trying to find my way."

Lately, since my mind's been clearer, I've felt it fit to lean more on those I trusted as well as those who'd seen me at my lowest. Making the decision to get a home with Billi didn't break my bank too much since all I do is save up, pay bills and stay frugal, but the amount I currently had in my savings wasn't going to last forever.

Purchasing a home for myself was always something I refused to act on, mainly because it made no sense for me to be in such a big space all on my own. Upon meeting Billi, I felt like this would be a forever thing and the next big step for us would be making this move. She was damn well worth it, and I had no problem with admitting that.

Lately, I've been on this fuck the world tip, but the more time I spent away from interacting, I stayed plotting my next move. Fighting is everything I had. I hadn't said a word to Elon or my father in weeks, but something within me just screamed that I needed to get back to what I loved doing.

"A'ight big dawg, that's the money calling. Lemme get to this shit, and I'm fuck wit'chu. Love you, bro."

"Love you too, fam, and thank you for everything. I appreciate it."

Reentering the house, I spotted my gorgeous ass lady up in her own zone and running her damn mouth on her phone. Just to see that smile on Billi's face, knowing I was the reason behind that shit, made me feel like I've accomplished something that meant the world to her.

All thanks to Apollo and his real estate agent, we lucked up with a spot ducked off in a nice subdivision out in Gretna. Our house was privately listed, which meant we had our own private yard, and it was gated off from the rest of everybody who stayed in the area.

The house itself was fairly new, having four total bedrooms, three bathrooms, a kitchen, a dining area, two office spaces, and a two-car garage. Putting down the cash to even call this spot our own didn't even come with a hassle because after every win I've gotten after a fight, I would always put a few thousand off to the side for things like this.

I left things in Billi's hands for decorating and furnishing. Women loved that shit, and I wouldn't know the first thing about decorating. For now, while we waited on furniture and other things we needed, the majority of her things from storage were being moved in, and we'd both be residing at my apartment until we were officially ready to move in.

"Baaabe, I'm on the phone," she whined. "Dee, lemme call you back."

Snatching the phone from her hands and placing it onto the island, she hopped up into my arms with the widest smile.

"You know we gotta christen the house, huh?"

"Leave it up to you to ruin a serious moment with some sex," she joked, picking something out of my hair. "I know I'm a handful, but I really am loving this right here. You know you're stuck with me now, huh?"

"I wouldn't have it any other way. Just seeing that beautiful ass smile on your face makes my whole world just make more sense. Maybe my ass needs to start doing more shit like this, huh?"

"This is perfect, baby, I love it."

———

LIL DURK FEATURING Melii and Teyana Taylor's "Homebody" erupted throughout the bedroom along with candles dimly all over the room, ultimately setting a vibe like no other. Dressed in lingerie that had a nigga dick rock hard, Billi was breaking out all the tricks tonight.

Bending her over on the chaise, she held on for dear life while I delivered earth-shattering deep strokes, admiring the beautiful view of her pussy devouring my shit as if it was perfectly molded strictly for her pleasure only.

Admiring the way she looked back at me, Billi started to throw it back, soon matching my rhythm, slowly maneuvering my strokes just how I know she liked it. Judging by her moans, I was perfecting my shit and doing all the things needed to please her.

The sounds of our lovemaking damn near overpowered the music. Pulling out before I exploded all in her gut, I got down on my knees and started to feast upon her sweet nectar. She began to spread her ass cheeks, causing me to lick every fold and crevice. Sucking gently onto her swollen clit, she screamed out so loud that her voice had started to crack.

"Stop running away from me!" I growled, delivering a slap to her ass. Immediately, her legs started to shake as she began to whimper.

Flipping Billi over onto her back with ease, our lips were like magnets and moved in an aggressive, hungry sync. Sliding into her wetness once more, she winced and met my eyes. It turned me on knowing she tasted herself on my lips and tongue. Placing her legs onto my shoulder, she bit onto my lip and massaged her fingers in my hair.

"Why do you fuck me so good?" she called out. "Fuck! You're going to make me so fuckin' crazy!"

Not too much of a talker, I allowed my actions to do the most of the talking and judging by the way this pussy felt, followed by Billi now being speechless, I was doing a damn good job. As I deepened my strokes, my dick immediately became drenched in her juices, which only meant one thing.

Completely satisfied, I went even deeper as my nut shot off in her with her reaching her climax. With her low eyes, we remained in the same position. Licking around her nipples and planting kisses along her neck, I worked my way up to her lips. Giggling through our kissing, Billi wrapped her arms around my neck.

"You done got us a house, and now you trying to put a baby off in me?"

"Are you ovulating?"

"Look at you sounding all knowledgeable and shit," she teased. "But thankfully, no, I'm not. However, we do need to shower because we did some serious fuckin' just now."

Though I didn't want this moment to end, she had a point. Billi went to shower, and I removed the soiled sheets and went to throw them into the washer. As I traveled to the kitchen hoping to whip up a midnight snack, my attention was caught by knocking on my door.

"Who the fuck?"

Ignoring the shit out of whoever was behind that damn door, I grabbed a thing of golden Oreos from the pantry with a cup of milk and then traveled back to the bedroom.

"Boog!"

By the time I sat on my ass, I didn't even feel like putting no sheets on the bed. Wiping crumbs from my mouth, I walked over to the bathroom and opened the door.

"Babe?"

"I'm just getting some fresh sheets for the bed."

"Am I tripping, or somebody was at the door knocking?"

"Don't worry about it."

Things switched gears, and after we both cleaned up, along with straightening the bed, we were both laid up watching old reruns of *Love & Hip Hop Atlanta*. After dropping dick on Billi once more, she was dozing off, but swore to God she wasn't falling asleep.

A commercial started to play, and as I glanced down, I

could see Billi was snoring softly. Bending down to press my lips to her forehead, I leaned over to turn off the light, and out the blue, there was that damn knocking again. By this time, it was around 1:30 a.m., and the noise must have woken Billi up because she started to squirm and then look at me.

"Who the fuck is that?"

"Chill, chill, lemme go handle it, and you get yourself some sleep. A'ight?"

"Yeah, you go 'head and do that before I cut the fuck up on whoever it is at that damn door. It's too late for all of this shit."

Highly irritated, I looked through the peephole and glancing at the sight, I grew pissed off.

Erial stood her bold ass at the door with a smile on her face like I'd been screwing her ass on the regular when I hadn't even heard from her.

"Whoa, nah," I frowned, backing her out the door as I shut it. "Fuck you doing here, E?"

"The fuck you mean what I'm doing here?" she questioned. "Stop playing and let me in, Kenji."

"No, you fuckin' outta your mind? Ain't no letting in shit. I ain't seen nor fucked wit' yo ass since December. Mind you. It's mid-June, damn near July if you ask me. You on that sadistic, stupid ass bullshit, and I'm not in the mood, Erial. All jokes aside."

"Kenji, you know it ain't ever over between us, so stop these games and shit."

15

Billi

Sensing some shit wasn't right, I opened my eyes and noticed Kenji's side of the bed was empty. Frowning, I pulled on a shirt and a pair of spandex shorts, refusing to ignore this feeling in my gut.

Sliding my feet into my Gucci slides, I left the room and traveled out the room to hear a small commotion coming from outside. My eyebrow raised once I heard the familiar sound of a bitch's voice followed by Kenji's low voice, which sparked something within me. Pulling my hair back into a messy bun, I went to swing the door open only to reveal Erial appearing to be in deep conversation with my nigga.

"Billi?" she squealed. "Kenji, what the fuck is this?"

"Boog, I was handling it and before you—"

"So, this is who was at the door, Kenji?"

Looking like a deer caught in headlights, before Kenji could open his mouth to speak, Erial took it upon herself to speak.

"This the bitch you avoiding me for?" She frowned, turning to me. "Billi, after all the shit we've been through, bitch you go and do some shit like this? Your own fuckin' homegirl!"

"Baby, don't get it twisted. You're my client. I saw how you moved, and I left your toxic ass the fuck alone. You were once my friend, yes, but now you're not," I pressed. "Now you're in my man's face why? Kenji, don't touch me because I'm a few seconds from knocking you in your shit!"

"Your man? Bitch, I know damn well you ain't fuckin' my nigga!" Erial yelled, turning to Kenji. "Talk, nigga! What the fuck is this?"

"Yes, bitch, my mothafuckin' man! My man who fucks the shit outta me eats this ass and this pussy daily, bitch, so yes, my mothafuckin' man."

Once those words left my mouth, she took it upon herself to swing at me. With my eyes enlarged, in that moment, I turned into a different person while I lunged forward until Kenji pulled me back.

"Did you really just try to sneak me, bitch? Mark my words I'ma fuck you up on sight, bitch, and that's a promise! I fuckin' swear to you, hoe! How the fuck you gonna get mad because your delusional ass claiming somebody who doesn't even fuck with you?"

"Nah, you need to go," Kenji yelled. "Get the fuck up out my shit!"

Successfully managing to push her out, he slammed the door with locking it, and the deranged bitch was screaming like somebody stabbed her ass. Breaking away from his grasp, I wasn't in the mood for talking as I stared at him and went into the bedroom. By the time he noticed what I was doing, I already locked his stupid ass out.

"You really on this shit? Open up the fuckin' door!"

"Nah, since you wanna open the door for bitches you used to fuck, you're sleeping outside. I'ma show you about playing with me!"

"I ain't even know that was that mothafuckin' bitch at my door! You tripping hard as shit, right now!" Kenji yelled, beating on the door. "Billi, open up my mothafuckin' door before I break this bitch down!"

"Break it, mothafucka! It's your deposit gone down the drain, not mine."

The old Billi would have pulled on some tennis shoes and literally chased this bitch down the hallway, but thank goodness, I was a changed ass woman. So, like the prim and proper bitch that I am, I locked his ass out because it was the right thing to do.

Scrolling through my phone, I jumped up at the sound of something hitting against the door. With a few more hits, this stupid ass nigga had the nerves to use a hammer to put a big hole in the door to get his way in. Not wanting to say a word, I watched his stupid ass poke his arm through the hole and picked the lock as he stood at the door, clenching his jaw.

"You really fucked up the door for what, stupid ass?"

"You're fuckin' childish! That shit was uncalled for!"

"No, what was uncalled for was you allowing that bitch to try to put fuckin' hands on me. I'm supposed to be your bitch, your fuckin' woman, and that stupid ass hoe had it on her mind to try me!"

"Fuck her! Now you let this stupid ass broad bring that negativity to my damn place like we ain't got shit to do in the morning. I'm not with the bullshit, so why the fuck are you letting stupid ass hoes like Erial get that shit outta you?"

"It's over with, and I'm not discussing this shit no more! Don't even think about touching me because I'm obligated to deck you in your damn jaw."

"Man, go yo ass to sleep with all'at yelling. I ain't got time for this bullshit."

"Keep on playing with me."

"You ain't gon' do shit, so shut that up."

Climbing into bed, Kenji turned off the light and pulled me into him. Removing his hands from around my waist, I placed a pillow between us and scooted to my side of the bed, which made him laugh. "You really serious right now?"

"Dead ass serious. Don't fuckin' touch me."

NOMI'S WEDDING date was slowly approaching, and the month of August would be here before we knew it. After the bridal shower, finding the perfect dress and all the bridal related festivities out of the way, it was up to me, as the maid of honor to plan the hottest, most lit bachelorette party. Hopefully, with the help of Diamond's assistance, we'd be able to knock out the remaining plans in time for the party, which was taking place within a few weeks.

"You've been glued to that damn phone since we been out. You good?"

"One of Kenji's old hoes decided to pop up at the apartment last night, and he's been sucking up to me ever since I left this morning."

"Wait, he had a bitch pop up at your apartment?"

"No, you know I moved out of my place, and we're now in his until we've moved everything into the house. I know I can't be mad at him, but the girl the bitch he used to fuck is a client of mine."

"You and your drama." Diamond laughed. "I swear if your life were a damn book, I'd read that mothafuckin' shit!"

"Go ahead and laugh it the fuck up. See, this is why

I'm always the single friend. I really don't have the time for this shit."

"Shut up because we both know you're not about to leave his ass. Y'all ain't even been together that long for you to be talking about what you don't have time for," Diamond expressed. "This nigga done bounced back from a serious injury and purchased a house for the two of you. You cannot tell me that his ass ain't in love! This is the happiest I've seen you in a long time, and I'm loving every minute of it."

Before I could respond, my phone vibrated with an incoming FaceTime call from Kenji.

"If I don't answer this, he gonna keep calling. Gimme a minute?"

"Of course, I'ma be over here by the bachelorette party stuff."

Walking elsewhere for some privacy, I answered, and Kenji's face had come into view, appearing as if he were driving.

"You ain't see me calling and texting you?"

"I'm busy, Kenji. I can't be staring at my damn phone all day. What's going on?"

"Well, I'm feeling some type of way, dead ass. If it makes any difference, I apologize for whatever the fuck it is you pissed about. I told you I ain't know the hoe was showing up, let alone coming at you like that, but you know if I would've touched that bitch, I would've been in jail."

"I'm mad because I'm a woman, Kenj, and I'm territorial. So, of course, when one of your old hoes calls herself popping up where we lay our head, I'ma feel some type of way. Have you been conversing with her?"

"No, Billi, I haven't. Last time I even laid eyes on that bitch was on the night I first laid eyes on you."

"Are you done breaking doors, Rocky?"

Showcasing that perfect smile, covered by his grill, that sexy ass laugh erupted, causing me to blush.

"You're the reason why my door is broke. You had me beating on my shit with hammers because you locked me out. I got some good news."

"Which is?"

"I'd much rather tell you when you make it home. I wanna see your face when I tell you what I gotta tell you."

"Well, whatever it is, must have you excited, babe."

"Fuckin' right, but I just got on this causeway with these no driving ass mothafuckas, so lemme hit you back. I'ma see you at home."

"Alright, I'll see you at home."

Since being in a relationship, I can honestly say all I do is make my money, hang with my same friends, and returned home to my man. Life was much more enjoyable when you stayed out of the loop.

Shit always happens to pop up out of the blue in your life, just when everything is finally coming together. I rarely even expressed myself to anyone, but this is the happiest I have been in such a long time. There were times where I would look around and see my friends happy with their significant others, and for the longest, I felt like I'd never be able to finally have someone to call my own, and here I was.

Thanks to Diamond's assistance, Nomi's festivities before becoming a married woman would officially take place in Miami, Florida. I'd taken it upon myself to book a fully loaded penthouse for all of us to take a load off. I didn't thoroughly know the majority of Nomi's friends, but I knew none of them would be on the drama for her wedding day.

"Boogie B! Where's yo fine ass at?"

"I'm in your man cave working on wedding stuff."

After a long day, I knew if I retired to the bedroom, I would have fallen asleep, so my best option was to stow away in Kenji's man cave perched in front of my MacBook. Greeting me with a kiss to the lips, he sat on the couch behind me and started to massage my shoulders.

"How was your day?" I inquired.

"Oh, you'd love to know, wouldn't you?"

Turning around to face him, he was cheesing as hard as a Cheshire cat. Removing his shirt, he still was smiling his ass off.

"Any minute now, K."

"As of today, your man is officially a professional boxer."

Like music to my ears, my entire world had lit up just by seeing how with patience, everything had turned out perfect for him. Kenji's been spending so much time wondering what his next move would be, and then this happened.

"How did this even come about? Baby, I'm so happy for you!"

"I decided to be the bigger person by contacting Elon and meeting with him. It just so happens one of his old potnahs was at his gym, some dude by the name of Remy Jordan, who's been looking for some new talent. We chopped it up, handled the legal aspect, I sent things over to my lawyer, and it's a done deal. Remy and his sports agency now manage me, Elon's gonna continue to train me, and we're plotting for the next move."

"Check out my baby-making major moves and shit," I cooed, climbing into his lap. "I'm so fuckin' proud of you. See how it's all be working out for you? I told you the chips were going to fall in the right place."

"You know, I wouldn't have gotten this far without you, right?"

"Behind a strong man is a strong woman always supporting and wanting the absolute best for him."

"I appreciate you. I know it ain't been easy rocking with my crazy ass, but I really wanna thank God for placing you in my life when he did."

"Boy, once you got a taste of this pussy that night, it was all she wrote."

"Man, listen at you," he laughed. "You better not tell that shit to our future kids."

My laughing ceased when those last words echoed in my mind. He noticed my staring and blushed while searching my face for answers.

"Kids?" I repeated, cocking my eyebrow. "Since when?"

"What you mean since when? I'ma marry you, and we gonna start a family. What's that y'all females be saying? That's that on that."

"You get on my damn nerves!"

16

Kenji

As a man, I needed to finish righting my wrongs. Various changes were taking place within my life to the point where I couldn't move any further without facing certain situations head on. Against everything I've ever stood for, I felt the need to put the bullshit to the side and finally have that well-needed sit-down with my father.

I started to ask Billi and Ameera for their support to be there physically, but I had to handle this issue on my own. The enthusiasm meter was way down, but this needed to happen. There were way too many amazing ass things happening in my life for me to allow this burden to continue to tear away at me. Ironically, today was the anniversary of my mother's passing, so I was really to myself.

Billi's day was spent catering to clients, and I didn't have anything pertaining to boxing on the schedule for the day, so it's just been me watching shows, trying to push my thoughts behind me. Not only was this day hard for me, but it meant a lot to me knowing the people who cared about me respected me enough to give me the space I needed.

Checking the time on my watch, it was getting closer to that time to meet with my pops. Already dressed, I pulled on my Jordan Retro 1's, grabbed my keys, and made my exit.

Leaving it up to him to choose the place, he settled on Deanie's. As a native to New Orleans, I heavily avoided the tourist spots at all costs, but this restaurant, in particular, used to be our spot as a family back when my mother was living. Maybe there was some sort of hope for mending our relationship as father and son, but I learned a long ass time ago that I could never rely on Theo Breaux for anything.

Right when I pulled into the parking lot, my phone started ringing with an incoming call from Billi.

"Yeah, Boog?"

"Ameera and I are at the apartment. Where are you?"

"I'm handling something, but don't trip, I won't be long. How's she holding up?"

"Well, after damn near dragging her ass out of her apartment, she's okay. I'm about to start cooking and we're probably gonna watch some movies. You know, girly shit. How are you holding up?"

"I'm okay, but I'll feel even better once I make it home. Oh yeah, the movers moved all the new furniture in too. When you wanna start unboxing shit?"

"Whenever you're ready, baby. The lease here doesn't end until…oh shit."

"Yeah, the end of this month. We gotta get a move on."

"We'll figure it out, but I'ma let you go because you sound busy."

"I'll text you when I'm headed to you."

"Be careful."

Sucking up my pride, it was finally time to face the music. Upon entering, I spotted pops seated off to himself as the hostess led me to his table.

I truly didn't know how to feel right now. Hopefully, today we would be able to find some common ground. I was in a much better headspace right now. I owed that all to Billi, though.

"I had ample enough reason to think you weren't going to show."

"Well, old man, that's the first thing we can begin to agree on."

"I know over the years we haven't really be on the best terms as of lately, Kenj."

"I spent so much time trying to be all that I could be for you, just to try to win some sort of affection from you. When I was a kid, all I ever wanted was the approval and support of my father. I don't too much remember anything about my birth parents, but I do vaguely remember my life finally beginning to have some sort of meaning once I became a Breaux. Mama would always say in order for us to live so great, you had to be away from home and do all of these things.

To be honest, that shit would always piss me off because I figured why in the hell would any man be so determined to raise a son when his career was apparently his first love. Then mama's situation worsened and you were nowhere to be found. She spent so much time trying to shield us from the fact that you were fucking around on her, and even when her own body was betraying her, you weren't there, man. Football was always first, and we came second, one of the many reasons why I hate that stupid fuckin' sport with everything in me. You tried to mold me to be your all American ass son, and I hated that shit."

"Kenji, I—"

"I've listened to you my whole life, but now it's time for you to listen to me, pops. That shit fucked me up. It turned me cold. It made me hate you with everything I had in me. Mama tried her hardest to get me to relinquish that anger and somehow make amends with you, but you didn't even make an effort. When she left this earth, it made me angry because I felt God should've taken you instead. Mama made me feel so much love that I felt I could do anything just as long as I had her at my side. Even when I believed I would get abandoned again, she made sure I never felt alone or disowned.

However, you, pops, you never ever once asked yourself that maybe your son, your kids needed you more than those coaches, those teammates, and everything else. You ask me why I'm so angry. Well, there you have it because after I was taken into your home as your own, that same abandonment still lingers. Even at twenty-five, that same ass feeling that's been with me damn near my whole life will follow me probably forever, and that's something that you'll have to live with."

Just as I expected, once I stated my piece, my pops sat there speechless. He probably didn't expect for me to truly tell him how I felt after all these years, but it was time out for that. I was tired of holding in my feelings on the strength of protecting someone else's, and that ended today.

Even after damn near crying out to this nigga, he couldn't even say a thing. Letting out a stifled laugh, I nodded and decided it was best to leave before I was unable to control myself. He sat there expressionless, still not saying a single word, and that is exactly what I needed.

"Nothing?" I asked.

Going the Distance for My Hitta

"I tried to be all I could ever be for you and your sister, son. For your mother, I tried to—"

"Try?"

Bringing attention to our conversation, I didn't even bother to apologize for my behavior. This coward ass nigga had his nerve. I found myself struggling with not putting my hands on this washed up nobody. Before I could do any damage and potentially lose everything I ever worked so hard for, I walked away from the situation. Ignoring him calling my name, I walked and walked metaphorically, closing the long, lingering chapter of our never-ending saga.

LAID UP in the arms of the woman who never shed any judgment on my fucked-up ass, I was extremely grateful. After the sit-down, I figured it'd do me some justice with possibly feeling better and not having that weight on my shoulders anymore. Unfortunately, I still felt angrier than I'd ever been, and that truly wouldn't leave my entirety until I laid hands on him.

Those thoughts will most likely never leave my mind. My state of mind depended heavily on those lingering emotions I often tried to block the world, my loved ones, and everything else away from. Those same emotions are what ignited my fighting habits, turning me into being the ultimate machine that I am on today.

"You never did tell me where you disappeared off to today?"

Climbing into bed, Billi positioned herself my lap, causing me to laugh because I had her ass spoiled as fuck. Even when I told her ass no, it wouldn't sit right with me.

She was rotten to the point where I needed to give her all she needed and wanted.

"You wouldn't even believe it if I told you." Running my fingers through her natural tresses, free of the weave, bundles, and whatever else these females used nowadays.

"What's wrong? Talk to me," she pleaded.

"I went and chopped it up with my pops earlier, and just as I expected the shit didn't go nowhere. Do you know this nigga had the audacity to sit up there looking fuckin' stupid after I told him how I've been feeling for all these years? It was a complete waste of my mothafuckin' time."

"How'd it make you feel after releasing that?"

"Besides wanting to beat the fuck outta him, it didn't do much. I still feel the same way I've been feeling, and unfortunately, I'on think there's nothing he'll be able to do to change that."

"Can I tell you something?" With a hint of uncertainty in her tone, it caused me to frown and caress her cheek.

"I'm listening."

"I'm always on you about steering clear of the people you'll need in the long run when I haven't spoken to my mother in damn near a year and some change."

"Why?"

"I blamed her for my dad not being there. I don't even remember him being in my life at all. My mama only cared about her career and climbing higher on the status ladder. She kept me in the best schools, the best programs, but she was never there. She relied on babysitters, nannies, and her mother to raise me. By the time I got older, I realized I no longer wanted to be under her roof and by her rules. My decision to move back to Louisiana upset her, and now all we ever do is fuss, damn near fight. It's a hot ass mess, honestly."

"How come you never told me this shit?"

"I didn't want you to feel sorry for me."

"Why would I feel sorry for you when my shit is not even together? Whenever you wanna get some shit like that off your chest, you know I'm here, right?"

"You're already dealing with enough, baby, that's selfi—"

"Ain't no such thing as being selfish when it's pertaining to you. I'm your man, that's what the fuck I'm here for."

"I remember when I first laid eyes on you in that elevator." She smiled. "I was thinking damn this nigga is so fuckin' fine, but I sure as hell don't wanna test him because he looks like he'd punch me in my shit. Now, look at us. You're obsessed with me."

"Just as much as you're obsessed with my ass, huh?"

"You love me so much, I can tell, but something deep down inside of you is just refusing to allow you to admit it. I don't know how many times I have to tell you that I won't hurt you. Until you start trusting those that care about you deeply, Kenji, you'll always feel the need to have to fight the whole world. Even those who do care about you would go to wit's end just to make sure you're in good hands."

17

Billi

"If you drop me, Kenji, I swear to God!"

Holding onto him for dear life, Kenji took off running like a madman, calling himself wanting to show out. In between screaming and laughing, I had to admit it finally felt good not to care about work, the big move, or bachelorette party stuff.

Usually, weekends would be my excuse to fuck off, eat, sleep, and basically be a lazy ass bitch without a care in the world. Leave it to Kenji to drag me out to the park a few miles from his apartment in a twisted ass attempt of us working out as a couple. Don't get me wrong. I loved my fat ass, these stretch marks on my hips, and my C cup sized breasts. Never having worked out a day in my life, I was currently catching hell right now trying to keep up with Mr. Athlete. I couldn't have my man walking around here flaunting his goods though and it's one of the reasons why I brought my ass here.

After running, Kenji carefully placed me onto my feet while downing some water. Droplets from his bottle clung

Going the Distance for My Hitta

to his lip along with beads of sweat falling down his abs and those tattoos.

"This is what keeps you sane, huh? Running around like you got all the damn energy in the world. You're the healthiest man I know, so why you feel the need to go so hard with working out all the time?"

"It ain't necessarily me going hard, lazy ass. I just can't stay still. The only way I'm locking myself up in the house all day is if I'm sick. I gotta stay active at all times. You, on the other hand," he spoke, purposely slapping my ass hard as hell. "You're blessed to be able to keep your shape, although I do see this weight you put on falling in all the right fuckin' places."

"You're sweaty, get back!" I laughed, running away from him. "Babe, stop it!"

To everyone else around this park, we probably looked like complete head asses running around like we were teenagers. I honestly didn't give a fuck, though. I'd gotten to the point where I didn't care what the world thought, and that alone had meant something deep down inside of me gradually changed for the better.

Throwing me over his shoulder, he foolishly stumbled and sent us crashing onto the grass. I laughed until my stomach started to hurt right along with my ass from falling so damn hard. Playfully slapping his arm, he took things up a notch with a serious case of public display of affection. Pecking my lips and kissing me lovingly, his lips lingered against mine. Laughing simultaneously, he helped me onto my feet and even took the time to dust me off from the grass on my matching Nike sports bra and spandex shorts.

"I won't even be able to do shit like this with you anymore," I pouted, wrapping my arms around his shoulder. "I still can't believe they're taking you away from me right after we move into our house. That's so disrespectful."

"I spoil you rotten way too much."

"Not enough, honestly."

Squealing, he palmed my ass and scooped me up into his arms, swinging me around. Holding on for dear life a second time, he stopped spinning and crashed his lips against mine.

"What's gotten into you?"

"I had just turned twenty-one when I decided to finally follow the beat of my own drum. For so long, I wanted to make my pops happy just to get his affection and hope that he'll see me. I stewed on that feeling for so damn long, not wanting to let nobody in or love me. Then I met you…and it finally started to make sense. You are what I've been waiting on…all this time."

"Thank you."

"For what?"

"Showing me the way a man is supposed to love a woman properly." Bringing his lips to mine, I held his face with a smile.

"Killa Kenj?"

In a split second, all the happiness he once expressed had turned to immediate darkness. Protectively holding my waist from behind, he stared unfazed by the stranger and started to size him up.

Judging by his attire and the way he carried himself, it didn't take much to realize that he was no stranger to the streets. Street niggas who were full of themselves often felt the need to be flashy, but that how you could easily tell who was the most obnoxious in a crowd.

"Ain't no need for hostility. We boys, aren't we?" He smiled, his eyes scanning over to me. "You got yourself a gorgeous one on your hands, K. How in the fuck you manage to do that? Last I heard you were fuckin' around with that broad who used to patch us up."

"What do you need, man? I got shit to do. You holding me up ain't gonna do shit but piss me off. Make it quick."

I could almost feel the heat along with the added on anger radiating from Kenji. Clueless on who the fuck this nigga was, I followed the strong feeling in my gut, screaming that something didn't sit right with him.

"You have been missing in action. I called myself being a nice businessman/ partner and waiting on my money maker. We got a lot of unfinished business, Kenj."

"Nah, I'm not in that business no more, big dawg. Now, if you'll excuse me, I got better things to be doing with my time."

"Who you fuckin' fooling, nigga?"

By this time, our backs were turned, but Kenji had stopped walking. With this looming, irritated look in his eye, he clenched his jaw and turned back around to face him.

"Unfortunately for you, Diezel, the world just doesn't stop on account of a stupid nigga getting fuckin' locked up. I'on owe you shit because I'm not fuckin' with that life no more. Do me a favor and stay outta my fuckin' way. It'll make shit a whole lot easier for both of us."

"Think about what you doing."

"And if I don't?" Kenji countered.

"You sure you wanna cause a scene in front of your lady, man? Judging by the look on her face, it's clear you ain't told her about the shit you've been getting into. I'd hate to have to be the one to—"

Unable to finish his sentence, Kenji was seconds away from hemming this nigga up, but once I caught a glimpse of the gun in the guy's waistband, I stepped in between them. That deranged look of pure fire lied in Kenji's eyes.

He was a ticking time bomb. I only had a few seconds left before he blew his short fuse.

"Let's just go home, babe," I pleaded. "We need to go now. People are starting to look over here."

"You need to listen to her!"

"Kenji," I urged. "Let's go."

―――

SILENT TREATMENT pretty much meant the wheels in his mind were turning devilishly. That night, Kenji went off somewhere and didn't even so much as send a message or give me a phone call. The workout had got it out of me, so once we made it home, I showered, and by the time I had gotten out, he was long gone.

Glancing at the time on the oven, it read *11:44 p.m.* Ignoring the urge to blow his shit up, I thought it was best if I just gave him the space he needed. Even with making that decision, it still didn't stop me from thinking of the absolute worst outcome.

What fucked me up the most was the tone of this supposed Diezel character's words repeating themselves in my mind. Kenji rarely ever spoke on his underground boxing life, but I knew it wasn't a pretty past. It was something he kept hidden, and no matter how hard I tried, I couldn't seem to pull it out of him.

Mentally, I could personally tell he was in a much better place. In a matter of months, the man I'd fallen hard for had gone from remaining a mystery to slowly showing me this side of him that I didn't even know existed.

After all, we were preparing for a new point in our lives. It would be the first for both of us. The uneasy settling in my stomach, courtesy of my nerves had me

Going the Distance for My Hitta

pacing all in the kitchen just waiting for his arrival. Picking up my phone, I dialed Nomi's number.

"Hello."

"Nomi, I know it's late, but can you ask Dri has he heard from or seen Kenji?"

"Uh, okay…hold on." Shuffling on the phone erupted from her end, while I placed the phone on speaker. "Billi, he says he hasn't heard from him. Is everything okay?"

"I haven't heard from him since we got in the park earlier, and that was at like four in the afternoon."

"Did you call him?"

"I'm about to. I just hoped I would luck up with Dri. Um, thank you."

"You okay? You need me to come over?"

"No, I'm okay. I'm about to try his phone."

"Okay, um, keep me posted, and I'll have Dri call him as well."

"Thank you."

Running crazy out of my mind, I tried his phone. Just as I expected, it went straight to voicemail. Shaking my head, the last thing I wanted to do was involve Ameera and possibly have her contact his father. That alone would be a recipe for disaster, eventually setting him off.

I could slightly hear the turning of keys coming from the front door, and within seconds, Kenji had entered with his hood on. Once he removed it, the evident bruise on his face was all I needed to know that he'd gone with doing something stupid.

Not even bothering to waste my breath with chastising him, I went into the cabinet to grab a Ziploc bag, filling it with ice. Sitting at the table, he flexed his knuckles, where I noticed the bruising on them as well.

Joining him at the table, I placed the Ziploc bag full of ice onto the table and traveled to the bathroom to grab the first aid kit. It all felt like history repeating itself all over again. Those high hopes I had of him potentially leaving this in his past had become broken. I felt betrayed, and honestly, I grew damn tired of sitting around waiting on him to end up serious getting himself fucked up to the point of no return.

Ignoring his wincing, I cleaned the open wounds on his knuckles. I could feel his eyes damn near burning holes into me, but I kept my cool in an effort of not to pop off because it would pretty much hurt his feelings once he heard what I had to say. Fuck it.

"Men tend to hide their emotions in an effort to protect themselves from all who they feel are untrustworthy. But with you, Kenji, you bury yours, and no matter how hard I try to get it outta you…you never let me in."

"This doesn't concern you, so I suggest you drop it."

"Gladly."

18

Kenji

"Judging by how you two barely acknowledging each other, I'ma put my money on it being some trouble in lover's paradise. If looks could kill, brudda, you'd be no more mothafuckin' good!"

"Y'all niggas are over here cracking jokes and shit. Get to moving some boxes! Make yourself fuckin' useful."

Apollo was on the chap shit. I loved my dawg with everything in me, but this heat mixed in with my not speaking to Billi and this new weight being on my shoulder, I was in no playing mood.

Today was supposed to be special for her and I. We'd bid a farewell to my apartment, initially moving all of our belongings into our new home. I felt the need to get an adamant move on since I'd be shipped off to Vegas for about four weeks in order to mentally, physically and emotionally prepare for this boxing career of mine to take off.

Physically, I hadn't stepped foot in a ring since my blowback a few months ago. If anything, I hoped that with signing on with a sports agency, it would be my golden ticket out and away from the dangerous game of life or death I had so willingly become addicted to. It was as if I had this internal switch that whenever I got outraged, I couldn't control myself.

Back some time ago, I found myself crossing paths with Diezel on some respect shit. He saw what I was about and immediately wanted to look out for me. I was a stupid ass nigga back then, though. Anything that involved a quick buck, I was always down, especially if it involved cracking a few bones or doing some sort of damage in the process. The anger I held from my abandonment issues, losing my mother, and never being good enough for pops plagued me.

During those dark moments, I got a bit too carried away. The thing with underground fights was that every match you won, you'd take home the loot. Unfortunately, if the police called themselves breaking up the party and in the event of that, some promoters got taken away along with the money. Diezel is a promoter, so whoever went home with all the earnings, had to give him a cut. I was a money-hungry ass nigga on the rise, so I felt like fuck it. I had to have been lucky because the nigga got locked up.

That day at the park just made my black ass realize, all debts needed to be paid in full. Nonetheless, leave it to Diezel's conniving ass to get me into some deeper shit. That night was my first time stepping back in a ring, and I damn near killed the other nigga. The earnings altogether were a few thousand, but according to Diezel, I owed him back pay and interest.

I was fucked, to say the least. Just when I started to make an effort to change my life around, the devil himself had clawed my ass right back in.

Billi was already suspicious and surprisingly not all at my neck with what happened, but I know it was fucking

Going the Distance for My Hitta

with her. The last thing we both needed was the negativity, especially since it would be our first night in our home.

"Are you compensating our black asses for this shit, folk?" Lando questioned. "The least y'all asses can do is keep a nigga hydrated! Y'all got me feeling like a fuckin' slave out in this bitch, bruh."

"Guys, here is some water for all the hard work!" Diamond stood at the door with bottles of water in her hands. "Kenji, Billi's asking for you."

Here we go with the bullshit.

Entering inside, I could hear her conversing with her girls, causing me to roll my eyes. Waltzing into the kitchen, all eyes were on me, and I so terribly wanted to tell these hoes to get the fuck out of my shit, but I kept it on mute. They took the hint, giving us some time alone.

"So, I take this as we talking now?" True to my asshole ways, I smiled big as shit, which I know only pissed her off even more.

"If I could walk around here ignoring the fuck outta you, I would!" she snapped. "Unfortunately, I'm living in this house with your dumb ass, so I have no choice. Your phone's been ringing off the hook. You might wanna call and let your bitches or whoever the fuck know that my patience is wearing thin."

"Whatever problem you got with me, you might as well speak up. We're both grown, so hit me with your best shot, B."

"I try so damn hard to understand why you do the stupid shit that you do. I pick my brain and worry myself crazy being supportive of your actions, but what good is it gonna do me if you're not even being honest with me?"

"What the fuck you want from me?"

"I fuckin' want you to grow up! You'on think I know what the fuck you've been doing. Out all times of the night and coming back here with bruises and shit all over you. Then you have yet to even speak on who you been out with."

"I'on gotta explain shit to you, no. I've been walking around here on mothafuckin' eggshells on the strength of protecting you and you coming at me on some hoe shit like this? I'on owe you a mothafuckin' thing!"

"And you know what you're fuckin' right, but how the fuck would you feel had I been walking around this bitch keeping shit away from you? That shit isn't fair to me, and you're dead ass wrong!"

"Wrong for what? Nobody fuckin' asked you to—"

"Don't you mothafuckin' dare turn this around on me! You can say all this bullshit, but you're not fuckin' fooling me. Kenji, when the fuck are you going to wake up? You got an opportunity to be better, yet you are out putting that at risk and all for what?" Billi chastised. "You spend so much time pushing people away that you don't even realize that the woman in your corner is trying to get you to see that this life is not for you anymore! What more do you have to prove? Why are you still out doing the same shit you promised me you wanted to get away from?"

I never in life had a woman call me out on my shit and make me feel guilty for it. That alone basically brought me to the realization that this really fucked with the one person who'd seen me at my highest, lowest, and damn near all the above.

Hanging my head down low, I stood there speechless and glanced up to notice the tears streaming down her cheeks. It hurt me to my core seeing her so disheveled, but this was my mess, and I couldn't drag the woman I loved into it. I couldn't even tell her I loved her because the shit frightened me. I was more afraid of telling Billi I loved her and potentially breaking her heart than I was of what could happen if I didn't pay this debt back to Diezel.

"Since you ain't got much of anything to say, maybe this changes your mind." Walking over to me, she slammed something into my chest, and my whole world stopped watching her wipe her tears away. "Congratulations, you're going to be a father."

The word *Pregnant* etched into the test caught me off guard. I always made a vow to myself that whenever I planned on bringing a child into this world that its mother would have the ring, and I'd be prepared. Unfortunately, I couldn't even be ecstatic or excited about this news.

"YOU'RE LATE."

Appearing like something out of a horror movie, this nigga had my black ass meeting him in an alley with not an eyewitness in sight. This was typical Diezel behavior, though. I expected nothing less.

Exhaling smoke from his cigar, he leaned against his Benz and started to laugh to himself.

"What's this I hear about you going pro?"

"Who you been talking to?"

"Nothing in this city happens, and I don't know about it, Killa Kenj. Judging by how late you out here, I'm sensing some trouble at the new residence, huh?"

"Kill all the small talk, man. I got what I owe you, and after this, we're done. I can't risk getting fucked up caught up with yo shit. I got enough of shit on my plate as is and running around with you ain't really on my palm pilot."

Throwing the orange envelope into his hands, what I owed plus gradual interest had been placed in the envelope. All thanks to Apollo, he'd taken care of the bill. He knew the type of shit Diezel was capable of, but the two were in two totally different tax brackets. While Apollo conducted his business professionally, Diezel was sloppy and greedy, always wanting what he was owed and then some.

"I'm very familiar with Remy, your manager. His father and I go way back. I'd hate to have to inform him of your illegal activities. I've heard and seen these beginner rookies step into the pro world, and in the blink of an eye, they lose everything. Even after all this damn time, you're still trying to prove a damn point to Theo, aren't you?"

"Like I said before, I'm done. Take it or leave it. And another thing, if you even think about firing back on some revenge type shit I definitely wouldn't follow through with those plans, big dawg. I got the shooters all around me, and I guarantee once I make that call…you'll be no longer. Nice doing business with you, big dawg."

19

Billi

Foolishly believing tonight would be a joyous moment of us finally spending our first night in our home, I wasn't prepared for the harsh realization, which was like a slap in the face while time continued to move and Kenji nowhere to be found. Turning over on my side, a tear slipped from my eyes. Staring up at the moon in the sky, I wondered if the higher power was finally repaying me for all the bad karma I've done in life.

Anytime a woman discovered herself to be pregnant, it was supposed to be an exciting time in her life. Those emotions were snatched away from me. I spent time all these months wishing and hoping I could be all that Kenji needed to change. Unfortunately, all I ended up doing was getting myself further involved with a man who wasn't quite ready to be loved. It hurt giving your all to someone just to figure out in the end that it would never be good enough.

Feeling the weight in the bed shift, I didn't bother to turn around because I could smell Kenji's signature cologne lingering through my nostrils. Closing the space between us, he pulled me into his chest and placed his hands onto my stomach, the gesture causing more tears to rapidly fall down my cheeks. The warmth of his breath tickled my neck, soon pressing them to the nape of my neck; I closed my eyes and started to savor the moment.

His pride mixed in with his abandonment issues just refused to allow him to vocally express himself. I hated not knowing what he was thinking. All I ever wanted to do was take all of his pain away in hopes that he'd be the man I know he was capable of becoming.

Unfortunately, the world doesn't work in my favor at all times.

Closing my eyes, I prayed silently, and after talking with God, I delved into a deep, well-needed slumber.

FLIPPING THROUGH THE CHANNELS, the majority of my morning had been spent lounging in the living area and sulking, due to having to cancel all my appointments for the day. Exhaustion hit at an all-time high as well, which put things into perspective for me.

I built my brand from the ground up with not a helping hand from a single soul, and then this happens. My pride refused to allow me to think or even be okay with the thought of a man taking care of me. If I was given the means to get it on my own, then that was what it would be. This was an unexpected event, but I know damn well what would happen under the circumstances. Then to add to my already highly stressed situation, Kenji still hasn't spoken or acknowledged the pregnancy.

The front door opened, followed by the sound of him placing his keys onto the key ring. I didn't even bother to

Going the Distance for My Hitta

look his way, but I knew he knew I was pissed off to the point of no return.

Soon emerging from the kitchen, he came to join me on the couch. Our tension alone literally made me sick to my damn stomach. I wanted to hate him. I wanted to slap the shit out of him for not even saying or doing anything to somehow make me feel better about our situation. I didn't make this baby on my own, but somehow, I felt like I would probably have to make it very evident to him that I would leave if it came down to it.

"I know you probably wanting to beat the shit outta me right now, and I'on even blame you, because I deserve it. I just needed time to…sort out my thoughts, Billi," Kenji expressed, eyeing me. "And I'm so fuckin' sorry I reacted or felt the way you disapproved of, but I wanted to enjoy all of you before we even thought about bringing a child into this world. I know that's backwards as fuck of me since I rarely strapped up. I got caught up in some past shit. I'm a pro when it comes to running away from shit, but…I didn't inform you because I need to protect you at all costs, B. There's a lot of shit you'on know about me, and I'm so fuckin' sorry for thinking my keeping it away would do you some good when all it's done is create tension between us."

Kenji still wasn't saying what I needed to hear. His words sounded sincere, but I was tired of begging and pleading when I barely even got the same thing in return. I went against all things I said I never would on the strength of falling for a man like Kenji. From the very beginning, I should have braced myself for this behavior.

What more can you expect from a damaged ass man?

"I asked Apollo for a favor to help me pay off Diezel, but I know it won't be enough for his money-hungry ass. We got a lot of history and when that mothafucka got locked up, I thought I was done with his ass. Somehow, he caught wind of my signing to become a professional and all he's seeing is more money," he continued. "I drove around all night thinking on how ecstatic my mom would be to know she has a grandchild on the way. It's bittersweet because no matter how hard I try to run away from my past, I know…I'll never be good enough. Even now, I feel like I'm rambling, but it's hard for me to express myself. I moved you into this big ass house, and you've expressed in so many ways how much you care about me and love me, yet I can't even bring myself to utter those words to you.

I wish I could be a better man for you, Boog. I really do. I'll be damned before I allow another nigga to luck up though. All I gotta do is stop thinking I'ma fuck shit up when all it takes is for me to just be the man my pops never could be to my mother. He took her for granted, and it made her blame herself. I can't help but feel like you're feeling the same way, and it kills me. I meant when I said I wanted to marry you and bring kids into this world with you, but I…I'on know the first thing about being there for you without fuckin' some shit up. Abandoning my child or you for that matter, I'on ever want either of you to feel that way. I always feel like when I got a good thing going for myself, God snatches that shit away from me. I'on know why, but it's always the same outcome when I think I got a good thing."

Pulling at my emotions, it ignited my tears, and without warning, they started to cascade down my cheeks. He then let out a chuckle and started to shake his head, fondling with his fingers.

"I'm supposed to be fuckin' excited about this new chapter in my life with the boxing and starting something special with you. I don't ever wanna hurt you or make you feel like I'm giving you half of me because I'm really trying, B, but it's so fuckin' hard when your backs up against the wall. I got all this pressure on me to be this man for you and I'on wanna fuck it up. I'on wanna lose you.

I just need you to be patient with me because I'm really trying my damn hardest. I'on wanna be the type of man like how my father was to us. The league took up the majority of his time and I've agreed to this deal, following in his same ass footsteps because I'on know where this journey is gonna take me. All I do know is that I need you by my side, baby. We can get through this together, but you just gotta be patient with me. All I ask is that you be patient with me."

Sighing and sniffling, Kenji's eyes met mine, and I could see the fresh tears coming from his eyes. All the anger, sadness, and confusion melted away once I saw his face. Just when I thought about giving up on him, he finally experienced the breakthrough I've been looking for. He let down the thick guard he's used to shield himself from all the things that caused him this never-ending pain. He needed me just as much as I needed him.

Climbing into his lap, I straddled him, and he nestled his face into my neck, holding me tight. His silent cries erupted lowly, allowing all those pent-up frustrations to disappear by the second.

Both of us were extremely frightened of what would come of this pregnancy, his career, and the next step for our relationship. I wish there was a way I could just take away all of these negative thoughts from his mind so that he could finally live free of being mentally and emotionally caged. As a black woman, I felt the need to love our black men harder because in life, you never truly knew what they were battling.

Deep down, I felt he didn't want to vocalize that he felt when anyone entered his life they'd just leave without a trace. It's probably the way he felt right now, but I know he wouldn't admit it. I knew what I was getting myself into and damn it, I was in far too deep to leave this man, especially when he needed me most.

FOR THE FOURTH OF JULY, we were invited to Nomi and Yadriel's for celebrating, but we figured it would be best to enjoy our last moments together before they shipped Kenji off to Vegas. Thankfully, the very next day, I was able to schedule an early appointment to confirm the pregnancy and see how far along I was.

"What this shit do?"

"Can you stop touching shit?" I laughed. "You acting like you have never been in a doctor's office before."

I could easily tell Kenji was nervously anxious, but after our talk, he has really been putting for the effort to being more vocal with me. I hated knowing he would be gone for four weeks, but according to Elon and Remy, his new manager, he needed to be in the right headspace mentally as well as physically and emotionally preparing for this new journey.

Plopping down in the chair beside me, Kenji was smiling so hard that his eyes were damn near closed. Reaching over to grab my hand, I laid onto the examination table and the door opened, revealing Dr. Willis, who has been my gynecologist since I moved back to New Orleans.

After introducing her to Kenji and answering the typical questions, she proceeded to prep me for a transvaginal ultrasound, which would prove how far along I was. A rhythmic thumping erupted throughout the room giving me goosebumps.

"There's the heartbeat," Dr. Willis smiled. "According to how things are looking, I'd say you're six weeks and a day. With the way things are progressing right now, I'd say the month you're due would be sometime in February."

"Around Valentine's Day?" Kenji questioned.

"Exactly on Valentine's Day. Wow, you had this planned out, huh, dad?"

"That's what I'm starting to think, too," I added, playfully rolling my eyes.

Having Kenji here to witness the one thing we were both so afraid of, it meant the world to me. I always said, whenever I did get pregnant, I wanted it to be with someone I could picture creating a future with.

Immediately after the appointment, we went to get food, and since it made no sense to go back home, I'd be driving him to the airport where he would be meeting Remy and Elon.

"I'ma miss yo mean ass. I can't believe I'ma be gone from you for four weeks."

"I wish there was a way I could come with you, but I know how you are, and you'll do great. The quicker this is over, the faster you can get a jumpstart on your career, babe. Are you nervous?"

"I've been joined at your hip for months now, so shit is gonna feel weird as fuck not waking up to you in the morning. I'on think I'm nervous about anything. I just feel bad leaving you. We just found out you're pregnant. I got to hear the baby's heartbeat, I'on wanna miss certain shit."

"I have another appointment when you get back, K, relax. Can I ask you something serious?"

"Shoot."

"How do you feel since the talk? Well, since you talked and I listened."

"Okay, I guess. I've been living with this burden for a

long time and expressing that to you, it made me realize I got a lot of fuckin' growing up to do, but that's something I'll have to get over within myself. You can't save me from the whole world, Boog."

"You're not your father, nor will you turn into your father. That goes for the biological one and the adoptive one. Fuck them. You're about to have a family of your own now, and I'm going to need you to be the best you can be for this baby and for me. Okay?"

"Okay."

20

Kenji

Most niggas come to Vegas to wild out, cash checks, or basically forget about their troubles from back home. Then there was my black ass, here for all work and no play. Shit, now that I think about it, I would feel incredibly guilty for enjoying the adventures of this city without my woman at my side.

All thanks to the man above, I left New Orleans on a good ass note. Despite our lover's spat, I felt comfortable knowing Billi finally had a chance to see how I viewed certain things. Some of those things being my take on love, my opinions on why I felt I was incapable of being these things she wanted me to be, and lastly, those emotions I kept locked up away from the world.

People took one look at me and judged me, just based on my name. They figured since I was the son of Theo Breaux, I would follow in his footsteps or some shit remotely close to how he lived his life. The only difference was, I am bold enough to follow the beat of my own drum. I didn't need my father's spotlight dimming mine. All of his fans, the people who loved him and all, didn't even know the truth behind the athlete. They didn't know the struggle he put my mother through, nor did they know he didn't even care to have a bond with his two children.

    I took pride in being the black sheep of the family because that alone meant I was destined to be great. I didn't need to follow the bullshit ass guidelines that were tied to this nigga who was my father. All the anger and hatred I've carried within myself over the years had done nothing but turned me cold to where I believed I wasn't good enough for anybody. The only person I felt who accepted me for my flaws was no longer here. Without her guidance, I felt lost in this world. It is the main reason why I turned to fighting. At least I knew the pain, hurt, and all those other emotions could be let out on someone I barely knew. It was much better than sitting in a room getting high, drinking or busting a nut in some bitch I didn't even know.

    Fighting was my outlet. It was my drug that I have grown addicted to. Nobody understood how much it helped me besides my mother. With her gone, I felt I would never find anybody to ever understand me or deal with my bullshit. Then, along came Billi. My Boog.

    She damn near made a nigga feel invincible. She put up with my flaws and even went as far as carrying my seed, which scared the fuck out of me. I didn't want to admit it to her, but I feared becoming a man similar to my father. I hadn't even popped the question. I couldn't bring myself to tell this girl I loved her, but I so foolishly had knocked her up.

    I couldn't be mad at anybody but myself because Billi deserved it the right way. I often found myself bragging to her on how I'd marry her and then have a few kids. She deserved so much more than what was offered, but I'll be damned before I allowed a nigga to luck up with mine.

Unable to sleep, I grew tired of tossing and turning. Removing my phone from the charger, I scrolled and went to Billi's number, cutting on the lamp beside my bed. My ass had to be up in a few hours, but I needed to hear my woman's voice.

"Baby, it's three in the morning over here," she answered groggily. "What is it?"

"I can't sleep, and I needed to hear your voice. You can't spare me a few minutes, mean ass?"

"You're in Vegas. You could be doing so much with your time, yet you're waking my ass up like I wasn't knocked the fuck out. You never cease to amaze me, Kenji Breaux."

"You like that shit, though. Aye, we good, right?"

"What's making you have doubts that we aren't?"

"I'm just up with my thoughts. You know I never meant to make you feel like I wasn't ready for this. I just want everything from here on out to be fuckin' perfect for you, shit, for us."

"It will be." She yawned. "You gotta stop this, babe. This whole feeling sorry for yourself and thinking you're never good enough. You're perfect for me, and that's all that matters."

"I really called to tell you I love you, B, and this world not gonna be ready for us."

"I love you, too, K. More than you'll ever know. Now that I got your love drunken ass to finally admit it, can I go to bed now?"

"I oughta make you stay up with my ass, but you lucky I gotta be up at five."

"What time is it over there?"

"One something, y'all two hours ahead of us back at home."

"Lucky you. Good luck tomorrow."

"I appreciate you, babe. I'ma let you get some rest. I'ma call you at a better time tomorrow, or you call me, whichever one you want. Don't miss me too much."

"I won't. I love you."

"I love you, too."

EACH DAY, I was given a new task to test my mentality and strength. Any other nigga would have cracked under pressure. Shit, I was damn near close, but what kept me going was each day that passed, I was closer to making it home to Billi.

"It's day three," Elon announced. "How are you feeling so far?"

"This ice bath is pretty much easing that pain, OG. I ain't felt this bad since ole boy whooped my ass last time I stepped in a ring. Remy's gonna be on this shit the whole time I'm here?"

"Compared to these big-timers, you a rook, and you're out of shape. We need you to shed that body fat, but most importantly, we gotta train that mental as well. How's the misses doing back at the new home?"

"She loves that shit. I'm glad I decided to finally get myself a crib. I just never thought I'd be this far with somebody like Billi. Before I left, pretty much the day after we moved in, she told me was pregnant."

"I never thought I'd see the day. Congratulations, son. Bringing children into this world is God's greatest gift. When are you going to pop that question? You know how I get. I'm old school."

"I know, but it's coming. Shit, I owe it to her."

"Anybody who willing to put up with the shit deserves the fuckin' world if you ask me. Overall, I'm real proud of you, Kenj. Your mother would be so proud to see how far you've come."

"If only she were here to see it all."

"She's watching you, every step of the way."

21

Billi

"Baby, if you're sleepy, I can call you tomorrow. I ain't doing shit but working on some new nail designs for my Instagram page."

"I'on care if you were putting nails on them client ass hoes you got, I ain't hear from you all day, so I'ma sit my black ass on this phone, and you not gonna say shit."

One week had passed. With splitting my time between work, preparing for Nomi's nuptials, and sleeping my ass off, it was safe to say I rarely was given enough wiggle room to worry about Kenji. We took turns calling each other from the time the sun rose until it went down. If neither one of us were able to get to the phone, messages did the trick as well.

I could tell they were working the shit out of my baby. Whenever he called, I heard the exhaustion in his voice, and at night, he could barely keep his eyes open during our FaceTime calls. On this particular night, he decided to be stubborn with not wanting to hang up. I know he missed me just as much as I missed him, but this step needed to happen in order for him to finally follow his own path.

"I stepped down with planning the bachelorette party."

"Fuck you do that for? You pregnant, not handicapped."

"I really see no sense in it. I won't even be able to drink or enjoy myself. Not that I'm upset because I can't do those things, but it'll pretty much defeat the purpose with my being there." I shrugged. "I'm still going to go and support Nomi, but Yanna stepped in, and she's going to take over."

"Them hoes better not make you feel no different. They just don't know you carrying gold in that womb, girl."

"That's right, baby," I agreed, glancing up at the camera.

His fine ass could barely keep his eyes open. Whatever they were doing to him, it had him exhausted. I wanted to hang up so bad, but he looked so damn handsome and irresistible.

"Kenji."

"Whaaattt? I told you I wasn't fuckin' sleep!"

"You need to take that bass outta your voice. I know that. My back is starting to hurt, and I really need to get some sleep. Call me in the morning."

"Hang up this phone, and I'ma call right the fuck back."

"Alright, fine!"

———

WITH SOME FREE time on my hands, a little retail therapy is just what the doctor ordered. I woke up at seven something in the morning, jumpstarting my day and knocking out ten clients with a few more left in the day. My next appointment wasn't scheduled until four in the afternoon, while I'd be hopefully finished by eight tonight.

People often talked down on my decision to go out on my own without bothering to ask my mother for a single dollar. I preferred it this way, though. I had a craft and a gift for making women feel better about themselves. Some may have thought it was stupid ass nails, but I've made thousands of dollars doing these nails, and the grind will continue.

I dreamed of one day opening my own shop, hiring a fully staffed team, and earning my rank as a boss. It's honestly all I wanted with eventually branding myself and expanding all over the country. I never vocally spoke on these plans because I felt nobody would take me seriously, but I was given a new reason to keep going, and that alone was my motivation.

Reaching for my dinging phone, I answered and laughed to myself. Going directly to my messages, Kenji slick ass had sent a picture of himself shirtless with my favorite smile. Damn, I missed him, but I was proud of him.

"Yo, B, that's you?"

Stopping mid-stride, I knew that voice anywhere. After all this time, I would have never thought I would ever see him again, but once I turned around, there he was standing right before me.

"What's up, Joey?"

Physically, he looked to have put on some weight and even looked much healthier since the last time I saw him. It has been so damn long, but I really had no ill feelings against him. I just moved on to something better, leaving him in the wind.

"Damn, it's been a long ass time." He smiled, scanning over every part of me. "How you been?"

"Okay, for the most part. What about yourself? You look good."

Going the Distance for My Hitta

"Going on five months sober. After our falling out, I just needed to find a change. I put you through a lot of shit that I wish I can take back, real talk. You ain't deserve any of that, and I wanna just apologize for that. I took advantage of you."

"Jo'Vaughn, it's cool. We both were making a mistake and as crazy as it may sound, I forgive you. I forgave you a long ass time ago. Plus, you have your wife and those babies depending on you. Whatever we had needs to be left in the past."

"You're with dude still?"

"Yeah."

"He's lucky to have somebody like you in his corner. You're a blessing to any man. I just wish I wouldn't have played such a part in fuckin' you over. I got a show at HOB tonight. It's for my album release. If you not busy, come on through, have a few drinks, and enjoy yourself. You can invite them judgmental ass friends you got. Hell, them hoes probably need a pick me up."

"I appreciate the gesture, Joey, but I can't. It'll be disrespectful to my boyfriend, and I'd rather not...and I do mean that in the nicest way possible. I'm sorry, but I can't. You have a nice rest of your day."

Never would I have thought I would be able to walk away from Joey, but I was no longer that girl. For the longest, I took pride in strutting around here thinking I was doing something right by sleeping around with somebody's husband. With a man of my own, God only knows the type of hell I would raise if Kenji ever stepped out on me.

I firmly believed in karma. I also believed that certain things happened for a reason. Joey and I were once like fire and ice. He was my drug. I felt no other man could appreciate me the way he did. But, the thought of having someone to call my own blinded me when he wasn't even mine to begin with. For some odd reason, I stupidly thought I would live this happy ass life with a fairy tale ending, selfishly not even worried about his wife or children.

Now here I was, almost in her shoes, expecting a child and in love with my child's father. I would kill if anything ever thought about ruining what we had, but I couldn't even bring myself to think of Chandler's feelings. I just hoped my karma wouldn't come back on this baby or in a way that would ultimately break me.

Deciding to cut my shopping trip short, I hightailed to my client's place of residence. Her name was Kyla, and she resided in a gated community. She stripped full time, but also happened to be one of my loyal customers. I actually met her through Erial, but that's neither here nor there.

"Oh my gosh, I'm so fuckin' glad you were able to squeeze me in!" Kyla explained. "Girl, how you been?"

"Working my damn ass off. I recently just moved to Gretna with my boyfriend, so I can't complain."

The majority of my clients were self-made bosses of their own. I was a firm believer in women openly being able to do whatever they preferred to earn their coin.

I could remember back when I first started doing nails, how people used to clown the fuck out of me for taking something like this so serious. Little did they know I was plotting to build up my own brand. Down the line of finding my way, I crossed paths with some good people and others, not so great.

In an industry like this one, you had to deal with competitive bitches and naysayers who refused to believe that you would make it out. For so long, I spent being known as Billi Samuels, the fatherless daughter to Shiba Samuels, the celebrity stylist who has worked with all celebrities around the world. I just needed to prove them all wrong.

"You know I don't do the drama shit, but in the club the other night, I heard some of the girls saying how you and Erial are beefed out. They're refusing to use your services, but they just don't know I'm always loyal to my homegirl."

"Erial's full of shit just like the rest of them bitches. It ain't nothing but he say/ she say."

"That's what the fuck I'm talking about, girl. Fuck them hoes. Anyway, you seem to be doing good for yourself. Do I hear wedding bells soon?"

"We'll see. How have things been at the club?"

"Tiring, I never thought I'd say these words, but B, I can't take this shit no more." Kyla shrugged, shaking her head. "I'm thinking about going back to school, a university maybe. It always what my mother wanted before she left this earth. The money itself is good, but this shit gets old."

"You can do anything you set your mind to, Ky, know that. If it's one thing I love, it's seeing us black women strive, no matter what. It's never too late for anything. Shit, I wish I would've followed my first mind and went when I had the chance."

"Why didn't you?"

"Rebelling against my mother. She wanted me to follow in her footsteps and shit, but I wasn't fuckin' with it."

"My mother not here no more, and I miss her so much 'til it hurts. You need to get right with her before it's too late, Billi. Real talk."

"I will. In due time."

22

Kenji

Taking a moment away from New Orleans is just what I needed for my mental health. Under any other circumstance, I would be living the fuckin' life out here in Vegas, but prepping for my career meant way more to me than acting an ass in Sin City.

The usual routine consisted of Elon's strict workouts created to test my everything. For the first few days, I would throw up nonstop just from pure exhaustion. I would have a match with Remy's top boxers and then endure other shit I didn't even know could be considered as a workout for an athlete.

The heat out here on this side differs completely from the humid hot I usually deal with back at home in Louisiana. All day long, it was nonstop. I was given a strict meal plan and shakes to drink to maintain the proper shedding of the extra body fat. I have never been a major drinker or smoker, but with the way I've been feeling after these days, I felt out of shape as fuck.

Week one got it out of me, and since we were smack in

the middle of week two, the only thing on my mind was going harder, along with getting better each day.

Sweat coated my body, followed by an aching pain deriving from the power ropes. Remy was about to get popped with all this damn yelling he was doing, but I tuned him out. Next, he made the call for the tractor tire flips. The whistle sounded and grunting aloud, I pushed through the pain, soreness, and the sun's ray just beaming down, unapologetically.

Each day, something new was tested. No matter how grueling each task was, I fought through that shit with everything in me.

"Watch the combination, Kenji!" Remy shouted. "You gotta make him work, or he's gonna defeat you!"

One of Remy's clients, who occasionally used Elon's gym, went by the name of Zo. He was half Mexican, half black, and we were just about in the same weight class. He'd been in the game for about a few months but knew Remy's teachings by the book. I struggled with taking heed to direction because I always followed my own way and that's how I would always defeat my opponent.

Most thought boxing mainly was a battle to see who was the strongest, when it was only half of it. Mentally, you had to one-up on your opponent, both mentally and physically. It is a gift not too many niggas are blessed with. I've been fighting all my life with untrustworthy folks since the day I could comprehend certain things, but I'll never be stupid enough to fight just using my strength.

"There you go, son! Work smarter and not harder," Elon coached. "Plant those feet, keep them planted to strengthen your punches!"

Day after day, ice baths were required to help with the soreness. After a shower, I used the remaining ounce of energy to inform Billi about my day while giving her the same opportunity as well.

"Are you even listening to me?"

Just like every other night, I made sure to check-in and informed her of my day. The only problem was that tonight, I felt entirely too exhausted to even pay attention to her explaining what she'd done with herself all day.

"I'm sorry Boog, it's just been real brutal today."

"I'm so stupid, I'm so sorry," she apologized, shaking her head. "I'm too busy rambling, and not once have I asked you about how you've been these past few days, and don't lie to me."

"I'm good."

"You're not good, I can hear the weariness in your voice, and it's got me worried. Elon and Remy are not gonna like when I fuck 'em up, now will they?"

"You a fool." I laughed, eyeing her and shaking my head. "You know that?"

"All jokes aside, babe, I'm not liking the way you're sounding. You'on wanna talk about it?"

"I'm just tired, Billi. I am tired of Vegas, this damn dust, and this dry ass sun. I wanna come home so fuckin' bad, but I gotta do this…for us. But enough about me, how you been feeling?"

"Tired, all the damn time. I sleep on top of sleep now. You know they say the exhaustion is passed down to the baby's dad."

"Oh, really?"

"Mm hmm. I also gotta tell you something. Just promise me you won't get mad."

"You know that's what a mothafucka tell you before they piss you off. What is it?"

"I saw Joey the other day, and he tried to get me to come out with him. I turned him, down and I know it may not seem like much of a problem, but I just wanted to let you know."

"I don't want you talking to him no more. I'on care if he calls you by your full name, you ignore that nigga. A'ight?"

"Kenji, it was practically harmless. Please, calm down."

"This nigga ain't been around since I damn near busted his ass, and now that I'm outta town, he calls himself stepping to you. Lemme guess his coke headed ass apologized too?" I questioned. "Saying how he happy for you and shit?"

"Baby."

"Nah, no baby, nothing. I said what the fuck I said. Why you pressing the fuckin' issue?"

"I just felt the need to tell you." Billi sighed, rolling her eyes. "There's no need for you to be getting upset. If I knew it was gonna piss you off this much, I wouldn't have said anything."

"And you wonder why it's so hard for me to trust yo ass. Are you serious?"

"Oh my God, Kenji you know—"

"You might wanna just change topics before you piss me off, and I hang up on yo ass. Quick and fast."

"I'm not doing this with you. Don't even fuckin' play me like this is my fault. I'm not the reason why you got trust issues, K, and I really would wish you just man the fuck up and stop blaming your problems on other people."

"So, it's not your fault you fucked around with a coke head who was married with a whole family?"

"Fuck you and good fuckin' night, stupid ass!"

Greeted by the dial tone, things had escalated way before I realized my smart ass mouth was running rampant. Cussing to myself, I attempted calling back, and she declined my ass quick.

"Her mean ass is gonna be over this shit by the morning."

━━

ADMIRING THE SUNSET, another day's work under my belt, and for the first time since I stepped foot in this state, I felt like my task at hand has been completed. Of course, I still had a lot more learning to go, but I was damn near one step closer to getting the jumpstart on my career.

I couldn't even begin to explain the feeling, but for some odd reason, I just knew this was the extra push I needed to step away from the angry, battered version of myself. Spending nights just fighting because I wanted to see somebody hurt and in pain, it did nothing to me. The next night I'd be back doing the same thing with wounds and body aches, but at that point, it started to become an unhealthy addiction.

There were those people who relied on alcohol, drugs, and sometimes even sex to cloud those dark emotions they wanted to shield away from everyone else. With always being to myself, I felt no need to confide to a single soul or express myself because it would all be taken out in that ring once I delivered a beating to my opponent.

I'd made a deal to go professional. The stakes were much higher, plus I couldn't be out throwing my fist to any mothafucka who tempted my ass. Any wrong move, this could all turn sour, and I would lose everything.

Making this decision wasn't solely for me, but for Billi and our child as well. My worst fear was becoming just like my father. I wasn't too ecstatic about her bringing this baby into this world with us being unwed and our shit not being thoroughly together, but I'll be damned before I let her down.

As I thought back on the small argument, my hotheaded ass should have known better than to utter those words to her. My stupid ass just got upset at the fact she even mentioned this nigga, the same nigga who put her through so much hell. In my eyes, he was nothing. Fuck whatever both of them had, I would be her first and definite last.

"It's one of the many things I adore about this city," Remy announced, sitting beside me. "I've seen some greats come out here and be broken down, but eventually, they found their way as a true athlete. What made you wanna fight?"

"To be honest, it was an outlet I used to cope with a lot of the shit I didn't wanna face head-on. I started to get addicted to it. The adrenaline, it felt like power and when I stepped in that ring, nothing else mattered. I fucked with it, and it kind of stuck."

"Fighting tests more than your strength, young man. I don't know a thing about what you endured during your latter years, but you no longer have to feel like you have a point to prove. I signed you because I saw something within you that you rarely ever see nowadays. You have this natural gift to go all out. I've put you through hell, and not once have you complained, given up, or half-assed it. You know when Elon told me about you, I couldn't believe it. You showed me different, and I commend you, which is why I'm giving you a day off tomorrow. You deserve it."

THAT FOLLOWING DAY, instead of remaining cooped up in my suite, I used the opportunity of having some free time to head down to the jeweler. After searching online, I had contacted an owner who was supposedly the best of the best. I preferred to be alone, mainly because I didn't want anybody in my business, and this decision needed to be handled with no distractions whatsoever.

Once I arrived, the owner, Ross Vitale, was extremely helpful with the process.

"Your options are endless, plus we also have an option for you to personally customize as well."

"Nah, I think I'ma save the custom shit for the wedding ring."

Never in a million years would I thought I'd be sitting with a jeweler picking out an engagement ring for the woman I loved so deeply. I listen to niggas brag about this shit, but when you find that one, it's like you just know no other bitch could top that.

One of the things my mother drilled into my head was to always treat the woman you loved like she was your last. With the pregnancy, my career on the rise, and so much more, I knew there wouldn't be any other woman I'd want to experience these moments with. When our child entered this world, I wanted him or her to know, I sincerely loved their mother with all I had.

"What type of woman is she?" Ross asked.

"High maintenance fa'sho, but she's also a hustler. She got her own, and at first, I couldn't really top that. I just knew I had to show her my true self and just go with the flow. She's special to me, on the real. We also found out she's expecting, so I definitely don't wanna wait any longer."

"Well, you've come to the right place."

23

Billi

Nomi's wedding countdown had officially started. Using this time to pack for the festivities taking place in Miami for the bachelorette plans, Lord knows I needed this small getaway, even if it was for a few days, and I wouldn't be able to smoke or drink. To be able to openly celebrate with my girl is all I needed, especially since I needed the distraction as of now.

The month of July had passed, we were now headed into August, and after a long time coming, Kenji would finally be headed home.

"So, after Nomi's a married woman, the next one in the bunch is our baby, right?" Diamond suggested.

"Why shit always gotta be thrown back on me? This is not about Kenji or me. This is about Nomi and our last outing before our girl is a married woman."

"Fuck you mean, last outing?" Nomi frowned. "Bitch, you are coming to Miami. I still don't know why you allowed Yanna's unorganized ass to take over. That bitch is my line sister, but she the last person I need to be over my party. I'm still pissed, so not even you hiring a chef or having this good ass wine is gonna soothe that over."

"Why'd you step down again?" Diamond questioned. "You never really spoke on why."

After damn near a month of keeping away the good news, I figured this to be the perfect time to inform my friends of the pregnancy. With it being my first, I wanted everything to be smooth sailing. I've successfully hit my tenth-week mark, and they were both beginning to get questionable as to why the life of the party was no longer drinking or having the occasional blunt every so often.

"Since I can't keep shit from either one of you bitches, I guess it's time I finally decided to come clean."

Grabbing the step stool and reaching on top of the fridge, I grabbed the two gift bags containing a customized wine glass, reading, *Drink for Mommy, she won't be free 'til February*.

"Bitch, what is this?" Nomi laughed.

"Can we open it?" Diamond questioned.

"Yeah, go ahead."

Not even a second after opening the bag, Nomi's dramatic ass looked up at me with watery eyes, and Diamond started to scream.

"Oh my god! Oh my god! Is this real? B, this better not be a joke!"

"Please don't let this be a joke and you got my ass crying!"

"I'm pregnant."

Without even giving it a second thought, they bombarded me with hugs and in that moment, I knew they would both be here every step of the way. After indulging in our dinner, we migrated to the living area where we just talked openly like the group of friends we were.

"It still feels surreal that in less than a few weeks, I'll be changing my last name to the man I dreamed of having. Now the only one left is our boo, boo!"

"Have y'all talked about marriage? You always would say when we became friends that you always wanted to get married, then have kids."

"A little, but I don't want him to feel like we just have to get married because I'm pregnant. Sometimes shit happens out of order, and I'm completely okay with that," I replied, shrugging. "Speaking of things happening out of order, I saw Joey some weeks ago."

"Lemme guess," Diamond started, "He saw you and he had a come to Jesus moment?"

"He claims he's clean and wanted me to come out to see him perform. I turned him down and told Kenji, who flipped his shit."

"You and that man's personalities," Nomi laughed. "I can only imagine how much of an alpha this baby is going to be. You tell anyone else besides us?"

"Nah, I haven't talked to my mother in months, and you two are all I have. I'm sure Kenji's told his trainer and manager plus his sister."

"Once this pregnancy transpires, sis, you're going to need your mom and I know y'alls relationship may not be the best, so maybe this is the time for it to be mended."

I understood where my girls were coming from, but not a person in this world understood my reasons behind having such a horrid bond with my mother. The last thing I needed through this pregnancy was stress and choosing not to inform her would be the best way I could smoothly go through these months.

The night had gone better than I imagined with sharing my good news with the two who were the closest to me. After straightening up downstairs, I started to run my bath water, adding bubbles for the extra needed relaxation.

Cutting off the lights and lighting candles around the tub, I took things up a notch by playing my R&B playlist, curated with some of my favorite songs.

Corrine Bailey Rae's softly "Like A Star" played from the soundbar as I lowered myself into the bubble-filled tub. The beginning lyrics brought me back to the very first time I laid eyes on Kenji, causing me to blush. Though you could barely even tell I was pregnant, this baby was clearly the missing piece I'd needed to make myself feel whole.

"Four weeks too long without seeing my baby."

Opening my eyes, I turned towards the door to see my man in the flesh, looking good as ever. Beginning to undress, I met him as he stood at the tub and pulled me up to his lips, smiling so hard to where my cheeks started to hurt.

"What are you doing home? I thought I wasn't supposed to see you for a few more days."

"Your man did what the fuck he had to do." Kenji smiled. "You got enough room for me in that bubble bath or no?"

"Always."

⸺

"LOOK like you might gonna have to take the backseat on this bald-headed hoe convention, huh?"

Not paying any mind to this nigga's negativity, the only energy I had was to lay in his arms and hope to God this sudden exhaustion and nausea passed over soon. Playfully slapping his arm, I rolled my eyes and ignited his goofy ass laughing.

Tomorrow night, Nomi's bride tribe would be hitting the airport to head out to Miami for a weekend full of careless fun. With Kenji's overprotective ass now home, he's been on my ass with getting enough rest and eating properly. Once he figured out, I had potentially been overdoing it with my workload, he shut that shit down immediately.

Almost as if the higher power were on his side, this morning I struggled with getting out of bed. I couldn't keep my breakfast down, and I only had enough strength just to lay here, letting him baby my ass until I received some surge of energy to finish packing.

"You think this is what it's gonna be like these remaining six months?"

"This all new to me, too. So, you what? Bout three months?"

"Three months exactly," I yawned. "If this shit keeps up, I won't be able to get to the money like I planned. Damn it. We should've thought this over. I'm about to be down for so many months and—"

"Aye, shut that shit up. You act like you ain't got a man to hold you down. According to Elon, we about to be up in August. We are gonna negotiate and go over details later this week. I didn't wanna worry you with the news, especially around the time of your girl's wedding and shit, though."

"Nomi's wedding is only gonna last a day. Plus, this is our future we're talking about." I sighed, situating myself in his arms. "I've been thinking about a lot lately, and I think it's about time I ventured out with expanding my brand."

"Which means?"

"Finally opening up my own shop. When I get bigger, I won't be able to travel to people's houses with the baby. You're going to be traveling with boxing and…"

Stopping mid-sentence, he started to stare, and immediately, he bent down and crashed his lips to mine.

"I know you're having serious doubts, but this new to me, too. Just know we gonna be straight, Boog. I just know it."

I didn't want to admit it, but my absolute worst fear would be bringing this child into this world and motherhood pretty much hitting me with a reality check, and I ultimately lose my drive to attain my goals. Thinking back on my childhood, my mother was never there and well, my father, the nigga, didn't even have a chance. My upbringing was pretty much being raised by strangers, nannies, and everyone else who wasn't my mother.

I could easily remember being a badass, rebelling just for an excuse to get the fuck away from it all. It did nothing but upset Shiba to the point where she delved into work, ultimately leaving me to fend for myself once I got older.

"You'on remember shit about your pops?"

"No, only that he's locked up and not getting out anytime soon. I may have brothers and sisters out there, but who the fuck knows." I shrugged. "I just know I want our baby to have a better life than either one of us had. I want him or her to know that no matter what, we're always gonna be there. No matter how tough it gets."

"That's already set and in stone. I can't tell you the first thing about proper parenting, but I'ma make it my business to give my child a better life. Like you tell me, you're nothing like your mother just like I won't be nothing like my father."

"You think your mother would've approved of me?"

"Most likely, but mama was a lot of things, and if she wasn't fond of you, she'd def let you know." He laughed, mindlessly rubbing at my stomach. "She always used to say she wanted me to give her a grandbaby before she left this world. I always used to laugh because I would tell her there ain't no female crazy enough to deal with my ass. Now, look at me. I'm obsessed with you."

"She sounded like she was an amazing woman. Hell, she's done a good job with you. I'm sure she would've been ecstatic knowing her beloved Kenji finally stopped downplaying love and finally allowed it to happen."

As I fought the urge to fall the fuck to sleep right here, his phone started to ring, followed by our doorbell going off.

"Ameera's here. She gonna keep an eye on you until I come back. A'ight?"

"You really got your sister babysitting me?" I laughed, rolling my eyes. "Where you going?"

"Run a few errands with Apollo."

Over time I have grown to become the protective girlfriend. I've been on my own for a while to know when certain people weren't good company and although Apollo has been his friend for years, I didn't trust him as far as I can throw him. You couldn't exactly tell Kenji about certain shit though because he would catch a fit. Deep down, he knew I wasn't a big fan of Apollo mainly because you cannot continue to involve yourself with people who refuse to level-up.

"Be careful," I uttered against his lips.

"You stay in that bed 'til I get back."

Not too long after he left, Ameera entered our bedroom and joined me on the bed.

"You don't look too happy. You two arguing again?"

"Not quite. Can I ask you something?"

"Shoot."

"What are your thoughts on Apollo?" I probed. "You ever get this weird feeling that maybe he's not exactly who he says he is?"

"I don't agree with the way he does certain things,

that's nothing new. Apollo didn't have it so easy coming up, so Kenji says. Mama tried her luck with trying to adopt him as well, but it just didn't work out, and daddy wasn't fuckin' with the idea, either. I do know he's been there for Kenj through some tough times. Neither one of us can begin to understand their friendship, but he's good in my book."

"I just think with Kenji's career now it's not smart for him to be involved with the likes of a well-known kingpin. Loyalty will forever run deep with the people you struggled with, I do get that. But—"

"Things change when a child comes into the equation," she stated, finishing my statement. "I get it. I may not have kids of my own, but you two…you two honestly belong together. I haven't seen Kenji this happy in years. You brought it out of him and I'm getting a niece or nephew out of the deal."

"I'm overreacting bad, huh?"

"Yea sis, most def. He's going to be fine, and you are, too. Now what we about to catch up on since I'm here babysitting?"

"Shut up fool, but whatever you put on, I'ma be tuned in."

24

Kenji

"One thing I can't stand is an 'ole ass scamming nigga who just refuses to fend for himself, dawg," Apollo fussed, shaking his head. "I'on care what the fuck you say. You should've let me handle that!"

"Yeah, because killing a mothafucka I got beef with is just what I need right now, nigga. I paid the nigga what I owe him, so whatever he does from then to now, oh fuckin' well. I know how to watch my fuckin' back!"

I was pretty much screaming fuck my past. After coming back from Vegas, it was like I left my past issues back on their soil, with only the essential things weighing heavily on my mind. This time around, it wasn't about just me. I had a family depending on me. There was no room for fuck-ups, past bullshit, or any other negative situation threatening to come in between the plans I had for making this chance of a lifetime count.

"You can't put nothing past a conniving ass mothafucka, brudda. That's all a nigga trying to tell you. Your 'ole lady becoming suspicious?"

"I told her I handled the shit, so you can only imagine how I feel lying to her."

The truth was I did follow through with paying Diezel what I owed him but being the snake ass nigga that he is, it just wasn't enough. Countless attempts on his end have been made to get the piece of my success he always wanted. When we first started out, I wouldn't have even gotten my feet wet in the underground world if it weren't for Diezel. Unfortunately, these were different times, and I just knew the game he was spitting would be all bad for me.

Apollo was resourceful in many ways that not too many know about. I trusted my homie with every detail and aspect of my life if it meant some reliable protection whenever I needed it. My G had the shooters, and he had the means to get anything done just by the snap of a finger. Our bond ran much deeper than most knew. Whenever I found myself too far off the deep in, he would always step in just how I would back when we were kids.

"I'on know la' mama like that, but you gonna need another lie to cover up the other one."

"I ain't necessarily lie, I just ain't tell her the whole truth. Nigga, I got this. I'ma just have to catch his ass slipping."

"With a slimy snake like Diezel, nigga good fuckin' luck. Somebody like that, you never know what they got up their sleeve. You gotta stand ten toes down at all times. You damn near done up and became a target. Niggas see you shining, and they hating. They gonna wanna piece. It's either you eliminate the enemy or continue to be the bitch they want you to be."

"I ain't nobody's bitch, believe that." Reaching into my pocket to pull out my phone, the incoming call from Billi. "Yeah?"

"You okay?"

"Yeah, Boog, I'm straight," I replied, sticking up my middle finger at Apollo. He found the shit funny as fuck, so I walked off for some privacy. "What's good?"

"I just wanted to check on you, that's all. Don't forget you have to bring me to the airport to meet the girls for like nine."

"I won't forget, B, I know I gotta drop you off. Since we on the fuckin' topic, I ain't too hype on you going way out there and you've been feeling bad to keep it a hunnit."

"I don't too much want you out running the streets with Apollo, so we're even. And besides, I can't miss this shit. Nomi's my girl. I'll just drink ginger ale and keep it lowkey. I won't do too much."

"You saying that shit now. Make me fly my ass down there with y'all and cancel all'at shit."

"You're trying to pick a fight that I'm not in the mood for entertaining. When you coming home?"

"I'll be there in bout an hour, B," I sighed. "Relax."

"Alright, nigga, I guess I'll see you when I see you."

"You will. Aye, I love you."

"I love you, too."

Returning to Apollo, this nigga still laughing like he heard the funniest joke.

"What nigga? Fuck."

"Come on, man. We got some more plotting to do."

───

GOING AGAINST MY BETTER JUDGMENT, I didn't want to swindle Apollo to doing some stupid shit, but ousting Diezel seemed to be the absolute best option to eliminate all dealings with him. If it came down to it, Apollo already expressed he would have one of his workers take the fall, but the plan was now set in motion.

I would continue all methods of communication with Diezel, along with having him believe that I would fulfill whatever deal he wanted. In order for things to move in motion, I needed to have a well-needed sit-down with the devil himself. I'd be a fool to meet this nigga in some back alley type shit, so I agreed to it. The determined spot happened to be a bar, located in the Lower Ninth Ward. Pretty much as public as it's gonna get.

Spotting him in the corner, sipping and off to himself, I cleared my throat and approached.

"Well, well, well," he greeted smugly. "I'll be mothafuckin' John Brown. You showed your face! Aw shit, this gonna be good."

"You sure talking a lot of shit for a nigga who's been blowing my shit up. What you want with me, man?"

"Come on, you know that's no way to talk to the nigga who got you started. Have a drink with me, man. Yo bartender, lemme get Vodka straight for the killa."

"You know I'on drink, save the bullshit. I asked you a question, man. What you want with me?"

"You know better than to talk to me with that bass in your voice. I spoke to Remy, and he says y'all been out living it up in Vegas. He got high hopes that you're exactly what he's been looking for, which is why he recruited me to keep an eye on you out here."

"I ain't no bitch, I'on need nobody watching me. See, that's why we always clashing heads. You can't run me, Dee. That la' dude you found who was fucked up years ago, he disappeared a long ass time ago."

"Nigga, I made you," he seethed, glaring at me. "So, fuck all that hot shit you talking. You a mothafuckin' fool if you believe we were done. We got so much unsettled shit; I practically own you lil' nigga. Now you be a good nigga and just do as I say. We should be good."

It took everything in me not to knock this nigga unconscious right here, but it was too much of a liability. Imagining this nigga's brain leaking from his head being blown out on the concrete, it ignited that dark side. Whenever it was ignited, all bets were off, and nobody could stop me.

"I became familiar with this cat from the Seventeenth Ward. He goes by Priest. I owe him a few favors. There ain't no hope for his old ass, though. He ain't getting out no time soon, but he helped me when I needed that. Your boy Apollo still moving work, huh?"

"I'on count the pockets of no nigga. You got something you wanna know, how bout yo grown ass ask him yourself."

"Keep on talking that shit and watch I embarrass you in this room full of bystanders," Diezel warned, eyeing me. "Nigga, you ain't shit. I ain't scared by this persona, believe me. You help me, and I fuckin' help you. Remy tells me your first fight is coming up."

"Ain't no correlation in the bullshit you spitting. Get to the fuckin' point."

"Some rapper owes him, and he wants the debt paid in full. Blood that is."

"Who's the rapper?"

"Jo'Vaughn something, all I know is the nigga goes by Joey or some shit like that. Priest did him a favor a while back, and now he's asking for his cut. Now I know you ain't the killing type, but maybe your boy, Apollo, can help you out. You get the job done, and we're back to being partners. You fuck the shit up, and you got an issue with both Priest and me, but looking at it from my standing, you ain't really got no choice."

"You want me to off a nigga, and then what?"

"Don't make it sound so inhumane, Kenj, damn." He laughed, shaking his head. "You KO niggas on a daily. This should be slight work. All I know is the mothafucka needs to be dead before I have an issue. And we both know my light-skinned ass don't do no issues."

One thing about me, I didn't take too well to any nigga or bitch ordering my ass around. Fuck the shit he was talking; I was about to make this bastard eat them words soon enough. I didn't give a fuck about no debts he owed to another old mothafucka, and I sure as hell wasn't about to be dumb enough to risk my career on the strength of outing a rapper, who just so happened to be my bitch's ex.

Honestly, Diezel's dedication was immaculate. He was a fool to even believe I was on his side, but I was willing to do anything to make a nigga believe I was doing what he wanted.

Back then, I won't even lie, Diezel's ass used to intimidate me. He was some old light-skinned ass dude from New York and coming to New Orleans to run away from his problems. He was on the money train, and I wanted all in. I made a few stupid ass mistakes with trusting this nigga, but those days were dead and gone. I could not risk fucking up the future for my woman or my child all based on some old shit, so I did what I had to do.

I agreed to the deal, unknowingly setting this nigga for the kill that would ultimately get him the fuck up out of my life.

"All I need is a time and a place, big dawg."

25

Billi

"These Miami niggas need to get the fuck back! Damn, if I told these mothafuckas I had a dick, they still would try to fuck," Diamond fussed. "How much longer we gotta endure this shit? I have had it with Nomi's wannabe bougie ass bridesmaids."

"They're not that bad. You're just dramatic as fuck. I'on even know all of them, but this weekend is not about you or me. It's about Nomi."

Today marked our second day in Miami. After landing yesterday afternoon, all the ladies agreed to stay in and saving the turn up for tonight and tomorrow, which would be our very last day here. With Yanna now taking over as the hostess and all, I didn't have any clue as to what the plans were, but today, Diamond and I left the others back at the rental home for some shopping.

Nomi's bridal party consisted of her work friends, two of her line sisters, and, lastly, family members. I only knew a few since I have known her since my childhood, but I did know how jealousy can come about amongst friends, and with my attitude on ten lately, I needed to avoid the drama at all costs.

Truth be told, I was very excited to be out enjoying this moment with my girl, especially with her big day literally being days away. Lord knows I needed the distraction, but I did miss my man and my house, too. It looks like I would just have to suck that shit up, deal with these hoes, and show my support for Nomi during the best moment of her life.

"So, run their names down to me again?"

"There's Yanna and Noonie. They're Nomi's line sisters. Yanna is also the other maid of honor. Teal is her coworker from the hospital. They've been close since Nomi got there. Um, her cousin, Oriah, her god sister, Derielle, and that bitch, Kamry round out the rest of the bridal party. I'on like the hoe Kamry, but that's neither here nor there."

Thankfully, the majority of the women were pretty cool. With being a friend of Nomi's for so long, she introduced them to me, and I'm never the type to forget a face or a name.

"I could sense it, the minute we got there."

"Girl, back when we were kids, it was this nigga who liked me, so I let him fuck. I was a big hoe back then. At seventeen, I had that nigga paying my phone bill, he kept money in my pockets, and he was a hustler, I was in heaven. Girl, come to find out, Kamry started fuckin' with him on the sly and was mad at me after she fucked a nigga I was fuckin' with first." I laughed, shaking my head. "Fast forward to now, they're together and got like two kids. I think boys. Last I heard the nigga was fighting a murder charge, so there's that."

"See, I'm glad I met Nomi through you because had I would've met y'all when we were kids, hoes like that would've got the business. Period. I'on play that fuckin' behind me shit, especially if we cool. That's dead."

"Girl, I'm not worried about Kamry or the nigga now. She got the short end of the stick. Hell, when that nigga was popping, I wanted him, but he ain't hitting on shit now. Plus, I'm a changed ass bitch and I'm leaving the bullshit in the past. I think deep down that hoe just hated my guts because she knew I had that nigga's heart."

Just as those words escaped my lips, Kenji's name flashed onto my screen with an incoming FaceTime call.

"I caught you at a bad time?"

"No babe, I'm just out shopping with Diamond."

"How's your bald-headed hoe convention going?" He questioned.

"That nigga is so fuckin' disrespectful." Diamond laughed. "I swear that's the same shit Zyair asked me when I called him this morning."

"Stop it, but it's pretty nice so far. As you know, last night we had a chef, and we stayed in. I needed fresh air, so I asked Dee to come out shopping with me. I got you something, too. What's your day looking like?"

"It's raining, and it's fuckin' ugly outside, so I'm at the crib. I'on feel like going out in the mothafuckin' slop today. I'm on my antisocial shit for the day, and I needed to hear from you. This big ass house is quiet as fuck."

"I can hear it in your voice. You sure you're okay?"

"Yea, Boog, I'm fine. How you feeling?"

"I had a spur of energy, which is shocking since I felt like shit before I left. Other than that, I've been sleeping a lot and eating, which I'm pretty sure is normal. I miss you, though."

"I miss you, too," he spoke, while I plugged in my AirPods. "You need to bring that ass on home so that I can release this pent up stress. I can't believe I let you leave this bitch without riding this dick."

"You're so mothafuckin' nasty, dawg. Did you get around to finding yourself something to wear to the wedding?"

"I just told you it's raining, I'ma go look tomorrow."

"Kenji, please."

"I'ma go, man! I ain't even in the fuckin' wedding. I barely wanna go to this shit. But Dri's my homeboy now, so I guess I ain't got no choice now, do I?"

"No, you really fuckin' don't. Oh, babe, before I forget, there's this girl here, one of Nomi's other friends, but I know her because we grew up together. This bitch is still holding a grudge from years ago and still hating my ass. Ain't that some shit?"

"As long as that bitch don't fuckin' touch you, we good. I'on have no problem with boxing out no hoe. I dead ass miss yo smart-mouthed ass, on God."

"This rain got you feeling some type of way, huh?"

"Shut the fuck up." He laughed, smacking his lips. "What time y'all flight landing when you touchdown?"

"I'll have to check the itinerary. As soon as I do, I'll let you know."

"Well, I'on wanna interrupt what you got going on, B. I love you and I'ma talk to you later."

"I love you, too, babe. Talk to you soon."

THE SHOPPING TRIP with Diamond last a good two hours, and before heading back to the rental home, we grabbed a bite to eat and returned.

"Y'all arrived just in time. It's time to start getting ready for the day party," Yanna stated.

Going the Distance for My Hitta

"Damn, why didn't nobody call us?"

"No rush, girl. Y'all are fine. It doesn't start until three, so we're good on time, just as long as everyone is not moving slow as hell."

I didn't know shit about what to wear to a damn day party, but after throwing clothes all over my bed, I settled on something to match the strict attire policy Nomi had ordered for everyone. With a house full of women, of course, the entire house was in an uproar with people hogging bathrooms and figuring out what they were going to wear. Thankfully, I shared a room with Diamond, and we both were on the same page.

"I'on understand this white shit. Why everything we wear gotta be white?" I fussed.

"It's our girl's theme, so we can't complain," Diamond reassured. "Should I do the open peep toe chunky heel or sandals?"

"I'd go with the peep toe chunky heels, so your feet won't bother you too much. Be honest, am I showing?"

"You're only three months, relax and no. Just suck in!"

"Hoe, I'm not trying to kill myself or let my baby suffer. You need help with your makeup?"

"You know it."

WITHIN THE NEXT TWO HOURS, we finally had climbed into our Uber, late as fuck, all thanks to a few of the girls losing track of time. While everyone sat around holding their own little conversations, I was looking for the best lighting to send a selfie to my man. From the corner of my eye, I could see Kamry staring intently, and once I glanced up at the bitch, she diverted her eyes with an eye roll.

"Okay, ladies, first and foremost, I wanna say we all

look bomb as fuck and right after this day party, we'll be heading back to the house to get ready for Nomi's appearance tonight at Liv. But I'm not gonna run my mouth too much, I'ma let the future Mrs. Knighten take the floor with an announcement," Yanna stated.

"Playing into what Yanna said, everyone looks amazing, and I wanna thank each one of you for coming out to celebrate with me. Most of you already know the track record and I'on wanna cry, but…" Stopping mid-sentence, Nomi started to get emotional prompting everyone to coo and the driver to reach her a napkin. "This will be the happiest moment of my life and it means so much to me that y'all are here for me. But enough of the sappy shit, our driver, Mr. Cassius, is gonna take real good care of us today, so y'all be nice to him. And, let's turn the fuck up!"

Arriving at the day party, the DJ must have known he had some crazy ass bitches from New Orleans in the spot because he was spinning all the hits. I thought I would have been upset at the fact that I couldn't drink, but with the way I was dancing my ass off, I didn't even care.

B.O.G Vonnie's "Share It" blared from the booth, igniting Nomi and me to bend over, completely forgetting where we were at the moment. Diamond pulled out her phone, recording as I started to shake the beat.

"…*that dick big, sis, you gotta share it. Hold on Mykel! Bitch, if you throw yo pussy right, bitch he won't fuck wit' me…*"

The song soon switched to B.O.G Vonnie's "Can't Take That Back" and feeling the beat, I started to do what I do best while rapping the lyrics. Not even putting too much effort into shaking, damn near everyone egged me on, causing me to catch the couch. Having the time of my life, I felt something wet being splashed onto me. Snapping out of my trance, I spotted Kamry in the corner being held by Teal.

"This bitch really just doused me with a drink, dawg!" Taking matters into my own hands, I picked up the bottle and was about to go for this bitch's head until Nomi snatched it from my hands.

"Nomi, get your friend!"

"Calm down, Billi, and let's just go get you cleaned up."

"Calm down? You telling me to calm down, and this hoe just threw a drink on me when we're all having a good time?" I frowned, turning to her. "Bitch before the trip ends, I'ma fuck you up for playing with me and that's on everything I fuckin' love."

Causing a scene, I had to snap back to reality quick and fast. Nomi grabbed my arm, leading me to the bathroom, where it was just us two. Taking a look at my dress, it was ruined, and I smelled like Cîroc.

"Don't even look at me like that, I didn't even do shit."

"I know. She's drunk, and I guess felt some type of way when she heard you rapping that song. If you wanna go back to the house, I understand. This is all my fault for bringing her and I—"

"I can't tell you who and who not to hang out with, but your friend gonna get her ass beat and that's a promise. Lucky for you, I'm willing to do it after your wedding, but she gots to see me. I'on even know why the hoe mad. I ain't make the damn song!"

"You're so thoughtful." She laughed. "No lie, I dead ass wanna go out there and fuck her up for ruining your clothes. I'm sorry I even brought her. That's on me. You think you'll be able to keep it cool for the rest of the night and tomorrow, too?"

"If Kenji even found out I was trying to fight a bitch while pregnant, he'd beat my ass," I sighed. "But I'm not about to sit here wearing this Cîroc drenched shit. I'ma head on back to the house."

"You sure?"

"Yes, Nomi, I'm sure. I'on wanna ruin your moment. Girl, it's fine, and I do wanna apologize for damn near cracking that mothafucka over the head with the bottle, though."

"I love your stupid ass." She laughed sighing. "Can you tell that it's starting to hit me?"

"Lowkey, yes," I nodded, finger-combing her hair. "It's okay for you to get cold feet. You're marrying someone the day after tomorrow. That's big, bitch!"

"I know, I just want everything to be perfect. That's all."

"And it will be. Dri loves the fuck out of you, Nomi. I can't even begin to understand how you're feeling right now, but it's all gonna work out. Now get up outta your feelings and go enjoy yourself, I'ma head back to the house and get out of these clothes."

26

Kenji

This decision I was about to make could potentially ruin everything I ever worked so hard for or could possibly be the level-up I needed to finally close the chapter to my fucked up past, forever. Potentially playing with fire, I already accepted the karma that would come along with this decision, but at this point, I was like fuck it.

Ever since the sit-down with Diezel, I linked with Apollo and we've been plotting, just waiting on the perfect moment to execute the plan. This dumb nigga believed I was dumb enough to body a nigga who had ties to Billi but little did he know, this would all be turned around on him. Pretty much a body for a body. I understood how niggas behind bars conducted business, but this little event of demise would just have to be something Mr. Priest would just have to be okay with.

Battling with my conscience, I honestly reached a point where it didn't bother me. Diezel's been like a disease to my life since we crossed paths, and it was finally time to dead the relationship. The darkness within me needed this nigga to die the slowest death, a way that would make him feel every ounce of pain. I trusted Apollo with ordering his crew to follow and keep a close eye on him, which they executed perfectly.

This nigga had no family anywhere. He was a loner. The job itself would be easy, and I wanted a front row seat. Shit, if the nigga uttered some quick shit, I might just be the one to pull the trigger.

Boog: *We're leaving here in the morning, be at the airport at noon. I love you.*

Replying to her message, I powered my phone off and focused my attention outside. The gloominess of the night skies matched my mood all too well. The full moon lit the sky, creating this eerie vibe that meshed with what was about to take place tonight. All emotions dispersed. Never in life have I killed or watched anyone be close to death, but when you're pushed to the limit, anything's possible.

"I see that look in your eyes, brudda," Apollo stated, clearing his throat. "You sure about this? One call, I can get my niggas in on this."

"You questioning my ass like I care about this nigga or something." I laughed. "I'll be damned before I allow a bitch nigga like Diezel to threaten my future, man. I got too much riding on this major move with going pro. Plus, I just found out my lady's pregnant. So, you fuckin' right, I'm sure about this."

Apollo may not have understood, but I was on a different type of time.

Staring up at the moon in the sky, I know mama was most likely tossing and turning in her grave right now. I could give two fucks how pops felt in regard to my decision making, but that nigga's never been a supporter of mine, so it was fuck him, too. Once I crossed that line with you, it was over with and done. In my eyes, you were damn near an enemy, and I needed to release this hatred I've held in for so long before I blew the fuck up.

Pulling up at the block, I spotted Apollo's guys parked in the duck off around the corner. Eyeing Diezel's house, all the lights were off, and the driver cut his lights as well. Receiving the signal from Apollo, his dudes went into the house and did what they were pretty much told to do.

A coward ass nigga like Diezel had ties in all types of business, back door, mostly. He was a true scammer through and through, so hitting up his spot, was pretty much a jackpot win for Apollo's street runners.

"You think he gonna suspect it's you?"

"The nigga ain't gonna suspect shit when he's dead, nigga. You like this shit, don't you?"

"I breathe this shit." Apollo shrugged. "You, on the other hand, you're my family. Just know if some shit goes down, I'm willing to take the fall for you. You gotta watch your lil' one come up. But you gotta do what you gotta do, so I understand your reasons. You love her, don't you?"

"You know my heart was the coldest. I fucked these bitches and never caught feelings for no broad. I stood on that shit for the longest. She does something to me, Lo. Like she makes a nigga wanna do right. When I was in Vegas, I got a ring and I'ma pop the question soon. One of the things my mama always taught me was to bring a child up the right way. I'ma marry her and put all this shit behind, dawg. It's time for it."

"Real ass shit."

Even when we were kids, Apollo and I witnessed some of the harshest shit. Unfortunately, he was dealt a bad hand and wasn't given the life I was blessed with. He remained in the system until he aged out and turned to the streets. He worked his way up and now earned the title of being the most prominent and lowkey kingpin ever to grace the streets of New Orleans.

We were on two different paths, but we both made it out and found a way.

The chirping of his phone, also known as the signal from his guys, sounded. Speaking a few words into the phone, he nodded, and we traveled to the house. Remaining discreet, I pulled the ski mask over my face and took the lead with entering through the back, making sure no one could catch a glimpse of either one of us.

Using the gun, I broke the glass from the back door while Apollo's guy cut the lights from the fuse box outside. Stepping inside, I could smell the strong scent of gasoline. This bitch would be burned to the ground without a trace of nothing once we were done. Entering the living room where they held Diezel, I laughed to myself, seeing how they fucked him up.

"Yo, gimme a light, man."

Lighting a candle, blood dripped from Diezel's wound on his forehead. I caught him to the point where he couldn't even run nor call for help. It was the perfect plan.

"So, this is what it's come down to, Killa Kenj?" He chuckled. "Damn, I didn't believe you had it in you."

"You'll be surprised at what a man's willing to do when his future is fucked with," I smiled, kneeling down. "So today I'm living up to the name you gave me, Dee. It's only right. You thought you were a fuckin' smart mothafucka for stepping me, not only that, you did that shit in front of my woman, and that was oh so mothafuckin' disrespectful!"

"I didn't think I'd see the day a bitch would have yo mind gone. Judging by how she looked, I know that pussy immaculate, right?"

"Exquisite, my nigga. I'm addicted to that shit. She

does something to me, and I just gotta protect her at all costs. Protect my career, too. You a mothafuckin' nobody though, so nobody's gonna come looking for yo ass. This makes my job pretty much the easiest thing in the world."

"You're making a mistake, Kenj, potentially the biggest mistake of your life. You'on wanna do this. Put the gun down and let's talk about this."

"Nah, I'm done talking. Yo, somebody hand me a piece."

Like clockwork, the steel met with my hands. Wearing gloves, I wanted not a piece of my DNA being linked to this location. Checking the chamber, bullets filled the magazine, and I turned off the safety. Twisting on the silencer, without even blinking, I fired off two shots into his skull. The blood splattered onto the wall behind him and his head slumped immediately.

Goosebumps formed onto my arms, and that deep hunger I always knew lingered inside of me was fulfilled tonight, and it was one of the best feelings knowing I was in control.

"Take him to the chop shop and have Bino handle that. Light this bitch up immediately and be sure neither one of you niggas leave until this shit is nothing!" Apollo ordered, turning to me. "We got it from here, family. I got a car outside, ready to take you to the crib. Job well done."

"They'on call me Killa Kenj for nothing, brudda."

Though this night will be one forever embedded in my memory, I felt no remorse for the grimy fuck. Diezel's done so much fucked up shit, this was the only way he had to go, and I felt like the hottest mothafucka on the block for executing the bitch just like he deserved it.

FABOLOUS FEATURING Chris Brown and Teyana Taylor's "Us vs. The World" blared from the soundbar, overpowering the sound of Billi's moans. Gripping the sheets with one hand, the headboard pounded against the wall as she grabbed onto my wrist. Looking back at me with pure seduction in her eyes, she bit her lip, soon deepening her arch while burying her face into the pillow.

Raising up and crashing her back onto my chest, I pressed one hand against her stomach, she bounced uncontrollably on me, the friction making my eyes roll to the back of my head. Allowing her to take full control, I sucked at her neck. The temperature in the bedroom alone ignited our fuck session. I didn't even care at the fact that she was making me sound like a bitch right now, but I needed to fall off in what belonged to me.

"Aww, fuck!" Escaping my lips effortlessly, she took things up a notch and bent over, throwing her weight against me with this slick smile on her lips. Delivering a slap to her ass, it jiggled as she moaned out, throwing her head back.

The sound of our skin slapping violently against one another erupted throughout the bedroom, her juices coating my dick. Dripping uncontrollably, the muscles in my dick prompted me to dominate. Thrusting deeply, her toes started to curl, and within seconds, that pussy started to clamp down on a nigga, creating a euphoria like no other.

Busting with no warning, I slid out and right back in, deepening once. Reaching behind to place her small hands onto my chest, I chuckled, seeing that she clearly had enough, but I wasn't close to being done.

"You know what's next. You ain't no weak bitch," I instructed, delivering another slap to her ass. "Turn around and open them fuckin' legs. I ain't asking either."

"Kenji, fuck, lemme catch my damn breath!"

Nodding to myself, I got down on my knees and started to feast from behind. Helpless whimpers left her mouth as I sucked gently on her throbbing clit. Attempting to run, I held her thighs, holding her in place and laughing to myself. Licking precisely between her folds and going up further, I gave not single fuck as I devoured her ass like she was my last ever meal on this planet.

"You gonna do what the fuck I say or what?"

"Yess!" she moaned, nodding. "I'ma do it, baby. Whatever you want, just don't stop!"

Coming up for air, she followed my demands and laid on her back. Pulling my face to hers, she softly nibbled at my bottom lip. Her lips lingered against mine as I penetrated, drilling in and out, slowly.

"I'ma fuck your black ass up for teasing me." Billi laughed. "Uh fuck, baby right there. Oh, shit!"

After busting our umpteenth nut for the night, she got it out of me. Breathless, she laid on my chest as we basked in silence, pretty much putting the icing on the celebration for finally having my woman back home in my arms. I didn't want to admit it, but I didn't even want her around the rest of them hoes, especially if it was bitches I didn't know.

It was true I was overprotective, but I had my reasons.

"So, all it takes is for me to be gone for a few days for you to drop dick like that?" Billi questioned, her small fingers tracing the tattoos on my chest.

"Marry me."

Sitting up straight, she held the sheet to her bare chest. Eyeing me with her eyebrow raised, she opened her mouth to speak and couldn't say a thing. My ass was probably still on a high from the sex, but I was serious, and I needed her to know.

"Kenji, I know my pussy is good and all, but you'on play like that. Are you serious?"

"You always think this shit's for giggles. I see I gotta prove shit to yo ass."

Not even giving it thought or using the time to practice a speech, I just went off the dome. Reaching over into my night stand where the ring been stashed since I came home from Vegas, it was the perfect spot because I didn't have a nosey ass woman on my hands. She respected my privacy.

Retrieving the box, I opened it, and the expression on her face was practically priceless. Her eyes lit up as she held her hands to her mouth, starting to tear up. Meeting my eyes, she sighed and started to settle her breathing.

"I ain't got no fancy ass speech or nothing because you know what the fuck you mean to me. I haven't felt this alive in so long and I owe it all to you, B. I can't picture myself even coming this far if it weren't for you staying on my ass and showing me that…all a nigga needs is a real rider in his corner. You've been that for me and so much more. Our child is so blessed and he or she doesn't even know it yet. I love you and I wanna spend the rest of my life with you. Say you'll marry me."

"Yes," she cried nodding. "Yes, I'll marry you, baby."

27

Billi

During a wedding, the celebration itself wouldn't be grand without the bride raising hell on damn near everyone who tried to lend a helping hand. As the maid of honor, I had to make sure everything was in place, but I was damn near about to freak the fuck out right along with Nomi if I didn't get any fresh air.

"This is my fuckin' wedding! How the fuck you gonna tell me how I can't feel? Stop looking at me stupid and go get my fuckin' father!" Nomi screamed. "I'm not coming out this bitch until shit is how I want it to be! Why the fuck can't nobody see that I'm stressed the fuck out?"

I couldn't even begin to attempt to put into words the stress being placed on my best friend and how she probably felt right about now. Marriage in itself is a huge step, but this woman's whole life was about to change. As maid of honor, I needed to ensure things went smoothly for my girl on her big day. Looking at the faces of the other bridesmaids, they wanted nothing to do with Nomi's wrath.

"Can I get everyone to clear the room for just a few minutes, please?"

Earning quizzical looks from the ladies, they whispered amongst themselves, and some even were rude about it, but I didn't give a fuck. I just needed these hoes out. Taking their sweet time, I slammed the door behind them and pulled out my phone to call Nomi's father, Mr. Lem, as he answered right away.

"My Billi Bee! How y'all making out?"

"Hey dad, um we're sort of having a little problem with the bride. She's refusing to come out of the bathroom, and there is only so much I can do. We may need you to come on down to diffuse whatever the problem is."

"Alright, I'm on my way."

Hanging up the phone, I went to knock at the door and place my ear close to hear her sniffling.

"Nomi, it's me. I had everyone leave for a few minutes. I'ma need you to tell me what's going on, boo. It's just you and me."

"Billi, what the fuck am I doing?" She sobbed. "Why does it feel like I'm making the biggest mistake of my fuckin' life!"

"You need to get out of that negativity, Nomi. This is a special day for you. This won't be a mistake, and it's okay that you have cold feet, but this is your man we're talking about, girl. Yadriel loves you so much. This is the day we dreamed about, and you deserve every bit of it. I called dad for you and he's on the way. I have some good news, but you have to open the door for me to tell you though."

"Fuck that, whatever you can tell me. Say it from the door."

"Is that the way you talk to the woman carrying your godchild, bitch?"

Smacking her lips, the locks turned, and the door

opened the door, Nomi's full face of makeup was ruined. Her eyes were reddened, and you could definitely tell she been crying for some time. Outstretching my arms, she walked into them and laid her head onto my shoulder. Laughing to myself, we probably looked like little ass girls, but if a hug is what she needed, then I was willing to give a thousand.

"I swear to God, you better not fuckin' tell me, he proposed."

"Surprise," I cheesed with a forced smile.

Laughing in sync, she hugged me even tighter and demanded to see the ring. Cooing, she fanned her eyes, causing me to smack my lips at how dramatic she was being right now.

"Billi," she whined. "No lie, I had a feeling this nigga was gonna pull this shit. Thank God he did it at home and not at my wedding because I would've had to fuck him up. But overall, he did good! How do you feel?"

"I still can't believe it. Even now, it's the next damn day, and every time I look down at this finger, I'm breathless."

"Regardless of it happening yesterday or three years from now, you know I'm all for just seeing my sister happy. I love you."

"I love you, too, you crazy ass bridezilla."

"Fuck you, bitch!"

After our embrace, a knocking erupted on the door, revealing Mr. Lem, whom I called my dad since he has been like a father to me. Me and Nomi's history as best friends dates back to years ago when I didn't even have a single soul to depend on. My bond with my mother was severely strained to a point of no return, so I leaned on Nomi's family for the avid support.

"My two favorite girls! How's my bride-to-be?"

"About to lose her damn mind. I'll give you two some time alone."

Grabbing my phone, I made my exit and assured the ladies that Nomi needed a minute, but everything else would be running smoothly from here on out.

Sending a message to Kenji, I waited patiently and went to stand outside for some fresh air. Staring down at my ring, goosebumps formed, damn near making me want to pinch myself because all of this seemed like a dream.

Sudden vibrating from my phone managed to tear me away from my thoughts, the incoming message reading:

Kenji: *Behind you.*

Turning around, I was completely smitten to see my man cleaned up nice. Courtesy of my working a miracle to that head of his, his locs were styled into neat, stylish bun. Attire wise, he rocked a pale pink button-down, customized dress pants that clashed well with the shirt he chose, and lastly, black Christian Louboutin velvet loafers.

"Damn, you fine ass mothafucka, you!" I laughed against his lips. "You clean up nice, babe. I underestimated you."

"I had to mob on 'em for the one time. Why you not dressed?"

"The bride was having a meltdown and needed a moment, so her dad's in there with her right now. I can't wait to get home and lay in your arms. Baby, I'm so tired, not to mention, this bitch Kamry is gonna make me fuck her up if she keeps on trying me."

"You can't let these hoes think they're trying you, babe."

"I hear you. I just…it's just been a long day, that's all."

Sensing an unfamiliar presence, it was almost eerie how fast my mood shifted from all giggly to be in the presence of my man to now looking over my shoulder, seeing the very last person I expected to be faced with. Anger soon replaced the excitement, the happiness, and I was left with this scowl on my face, which Kenji immediately sensed.

"Daughter, you ain't gonna even greet your mother?" She smiled, eyeing Kenji. "And who might this gentleman be? He doesn't look a thing like Joey."

"Babe, let me handle this, and I'll come find you."

"You sure?"

Nodding, he pecked my lips and eyed mama as if she were the scum of the earth, then politely had given us some time alone. She had some nerve showing up here today, but I wasn't even going to give her the energy she so terribly craved.

"You're doing better than I expected. Shocked the fuck out of me. Who you trapped?"

"I'm not gonna let you fuck up my day, Shiba. Not today, not tomorrow, and damn sure right now. I haven't existed in your world in damn near a year, so do me a favor and keep on pretending like I don't exist."

"Bitch, where did I ever go wrong with you? You know I blame that no good ass father of yours. That heap of bad luck on my back, but no, I just had to listen to my old, decrypted ass mother when she told me not to abort your ass."

"Sounds like a mistake on your behalf. Your words don't hurt me, nor do they bother me. I'm happy. I got a man who loves me. I'm in a good place right now, and that's much better than anything you've ever done or given to me."

"You have so much to learn, little girl. Just remember, karma always comes around when you least expect, and you're going to need me one of these days. Trust and believe me when I say it."

The old Billi would have most likely put paws on the bitch, but today, it wasn't about me or the problems that went on between my estranged mother and I. This was Nomi's day, and I was willing to put my bullshit to the side in order for my friend to have the best day of her life.

AFTER A LONG WAIT, it was finally time. The ladies gathered to say a final prayer, and then it was showtime.

The ceremony was decorated beautifully, and pretty much screamed Nomi. From the bridesmaids on down to the groomsmen, everything was perfectly picturesque. Walking down the aisle with the best man, Yadriel's brother, Yadriene and not to toot my own horn, but we looked damn good.

From out the corner of my eye, I could see Kenji smiling so wide with his nod of approval. Blushing to myself, I focused on walking down the aisle and taking our places, the entire crowd rose to their feet, awaiting Nomi's presence.

The door opened, and she stood there with Mr. Lem on her arm, looking breathtaking. The dress looked even better than I remembered it. Instead of playing the role of a modern bride, leave it up to my girl to jazz things up just to her liking. Showcasing her frame, some of her tattoos were also on display, but her veil was flawless. She looked like a queen, ready to marry her king.

Their vows were heartfelt, and it brought my emotional ass to tears knowing after all these two been through, they were about to start a whole new journey as a union.

Picturing myself to be in Nomi's shoes, my eyes scanned over to Kenji, staring at me intently, then giving a wink. Kissing my lips toward him, I focused my attention back to the ceremony. Nomi was emotional with all of her feelings on complete display for all the guests to see.

"With all the power vested in me, I now pronounce you husband and wife. Yadriel, you may now kiss your bride."

⸺

KINFOLK BRASS BAND rocked the reception hall, igniting a jumping second line that had the entire party cutting up and having the time of their lives. For New Orleans natives, the second line was a tradition for us natives during the time of a celebration. To someone who wasn't from here, it looked crazy, but it was just a bunch of people repping our city to the fullest.

It was somewhat similar to a line dance, but the moves pretty much consisted of gyrating with a mix of precise footwork, only the natives knew how to do. Joining the party, I had to kick off my heels as I held my dress, Kenji's crazy ass right was behind me with a drink in his hands, which had in fact loosened my baby up.

The band played their rendition Betty Wright's "After the Pain" and everyone were pretty much having the time of their lives, not caring about a single thing in this world. We probably looked like a bunch of drunken fools, but I didn't give a fuck because I was having the time of my life with the people I cared about.

Yadriel's folks were affiliated with the Indians of New Orleans, so of course, he had to show out as well. In dire need of some fresh air and to sit on my ass for a few minutes, Kenji followed me to return to our table where he appeared with a drink.

"This is my first time ever seeing you loose like this." I laughed. "Look at you sweating up a storm!"

"I ain't even know my black ass can move like that. I know I'd better put this fuckin' drink down, tho!"

"I could legit feel my mom staring at me from across the room, and it's pissing me off. I'm tired of looking at her, so I think we may end up leaving earlier than I thought. Only if that's okay with you."

"We a team. When you move, I do the fuckin' same. But you know what I always tell you, Boog. It's never good to be on bad terms with your moms."

It was quite easy for outsiders to think I just held this undeniable ass grudge when it came down to this woman. No one understood why it's such a hard task for me to openly forgive my mom for all she's done to me, but I don't think I'll ever be able to reach that point. The gradual damage has already been done, and once you burn me, I refuse to get placed in a situation where I'm burned again.

These times were much different, though. I've been introduced to the proper way a man is supposed to love a woman, and not only that, he saw it fit to ask me to be his wife. If anything, I wanted this child growing in my womb to be surrounded by love and something deep down inside of me, just strongly urged me to mend these open wounds. Unfortunately, I wasn't quite ready just yet.

"I'ma go start the whip so that we can head on out. You want me to wait on you or what?" Kenji questioned.

"You can go start up the car. Let me go tell the newly-weds I'm leaving."

Nodding, we shared a kiss, and he disappeared while I went to search for Nomi. Seeing me before I could see her, we shared a hug as she held my face in her hands.

"Thank you for being here for me, friend. I couldn't have imagined spending this day without you at my side."

"You know I got you, always. I wish I could stay and hang with y'all tonight, but we're about to take it on home.

Going the Distance for My Hitta

Mama's presence is irritating, and today has been long, you know my pregnant ass needs the rest."

"Oh girl, it's completely fine. I understand, go get that rest you need for my precious god baby."

"Hopefully, you and Dri can hop on getting me one of own really soon, huh?"

"Gimme bout a year, bitch."

"Alright, I'ma hold you to that."

Sharing another embrace, I instantly felt this omniscient force so great it damn neared knocked the wind out of me. Frowning, Nomi eyed me, and in an instant, gunshots rang out prompting everyone to crouch down onto the ground.

Bullets flew threw, the sound of broken glass crashing onto the floor, and everything literally started to move in slow motion. Breaking away from Nomi's grasp and ignoring her protests, the only thing on my mind was getting to Kenji. Running out of my heels, I felt another grip around my arm, looking to see mama.

"Billi, don't you go out there—"

"Get the fuck off of me!" I screamed, fighting against her grasp. "Let go of me!"

Successfully breaking free, I ran outside and saw the door to Kenji's Benz truck open. His body laid on the pavement, lifeless. Screaming out, I rushed over to his aid and took notice of the gunshot wounds coming from his chest and stomach, the tears pouring uncontrollably from my eyes.

"No, baby!" Shaking my head, his breathing started to become labored and, in his eyes, I could see the gradual fear. "Somebody help me, please somebody call for help!"

Focusing back onto him, I couldn't even bring myself to speak and reaching down to grab my hand, he opened his mouth to speak.

"Kenji, you can't fuckin' do this to me! Baby, you gotta hold on for me!" I begged. "Please, just hold on for me. I need you…this baby needs you. Don't talk. Just focus on me, baby. Focus on me!"

"Boog…t-they fuckin' shot me…."

"I love you so much, Kenj. I'm begging you, baby, don't do this!"

Cradling the love of my life in my arms, Kenji's blood plastered onto my dress and on my hands. Second by second, his life started to slip away from me, and I prayed hard, praying to God that he spared his life.

The grip he held onto my hands loosened, and I could hear sirens in the distance, while I stared into his eyes, somehow feeling like I just might lose my fiancée on this street…

TO BE CONTINUED

CPSIA information can be obtained
at www.ICGtesting.com
Printed in the USA
LVHW091614200820
663740LV00003B/547